Diaries of a Dead African

Diaries of a Dead African

Chuma Nwokolo

Gwandustan
2013

Gwandustan Edition, 2013

This is a work of fiction. The characters are figments and bear no resemblance to any actual person, dead or alive. Any similarities are fortuitous.

ISBN: 978-978-2190-13-0

Gwandustan Limited
P.O. Box 2260, Asaba, Nigeria.
publisher@villagerhouse.com

A condensed version of Meme's Diary was first published in Vol. 23 No 4 of The London Review of Books as '*Diary of a Dead African*'.

Cover Design: Vee Global Concepts Ltd.
Author's Photograph: Andrew Ogilvy.
Printing: Expand Press Limited.

Dedication

On 29th January 2002, my mother died. ***Eziogolibuno Dorothy Nwannefuluno Nwokolo*** *lived to read the first two parts of this book but she inspired them all. To be raised by her was to find, without searching, the most generous love of all. Nobody who knew her would fail to recognise her words in the better parts of this book. Those are the parts I dedicate to a woman whose praise name means: a good wife* ***is*** *the home.*

Only death could part her from her husband and inseparable friend, ***Nwachukwunedu Felix Chukwuma Nwokolo.*** *Living is a daily privilege to be his son, this man of character whose affections leaps the gulf between continents, whose presence ignites occasions. This book is also dedicated to my own friend and father.*

Chuma Nwokolo

29th January, 2003

Contents

DIARY ONE

MEME JUMAI

Occupation:	Farmer
Residence:	Ikerre-Oti, Delta State, Nigeria
Date of Birth:	June 5, 1950
Date of Death:	June 15, 2000
Cause of Death:	*Awaiting Inquest.*

MEME

1st June 2000

WHEN I WOKE THIS MORNING I was sweating like a slave on the farm. Yet it wasn't the sweat of hard work that wet my bed-sheet so. It was the sweat of fear. I was feeling as if a witch had poured fear inside me the way Ma'Abel used to pump our sleeping sons with pap, more than twenty years ago. If you see how my chest was doing! That my heart did not cut was a miracle.

As I pushed my door open into the compound and hung my bed-sheet where it became my curtain, I tried to remember the exact and particular reason why I was so afraid. I couldn't; and I'm not surprised. The problems of my life are not the sort that one narrates to a native doctor and he laughs before he starts his treatment. My problems are the sort that the boldest witchdoctor will hear halfway and flee. Is that not how I went to meet Catechist just before Easter and he said he wouldn't waste his time and mine by praying, that my problems had surpassed the kind that prayer and fasting solve. It's just that adversity isn't something people boast about; otherwise, in this Ikerre-Oti, no one can stand beside me.

It wasn't quite dawn, but, as Ikerre people say, only a ne'er-do-well needs sunlight to gather his farm gear. I got dressed. Nobody can call my house a mud-hut anymore, ever since I plastered it all over with cement. (Except those people who have jealousy and witchcraft running in their veins and they think it is blood. That type of people can never forget what is under the plaster.) On the harvest poles staked to the wall opposite my clay bed are the remnants of the 1999 harvest... *only three yam tubers...* As soon as those three tubers filled my eyes, the silence also filled my ears. Ma'Abel was *not* cursing her stubborn stove from her kitchen outside. Abel and Calamatus were not quarrelling over who forgot to tether the goat the night before. I was alone in my compound with *only three tubers of yam.*

That was when I remembered the exact and particular reason why I was so afraid, and my chest kept quiet. Because Ikerre people also say that the day a man recognises the disease that will kill him is the day doctors stop eating his money. I remembered the name of the fear that filled me like the urine of a witch; and when a disease has a name, at least it has a salutation.

His name was Starvation.

It was two weeks until harvest and tradition decrees that not a root may be disturbed in the fields before the day of the new yam festival. The situation was serious.

I untied my pregnant goat. Another week and the lazy thing should bear. I watched her climb to her feet and drag herself out of the compound to graze, scratching herself lazily on the broken gatepost. Just as I feared, young idiots with pails as empty as their brains were already hanging around the gate in front of my compound. They're waiting for me to come out to start their giggling and idiotic singing. They've left the water they were sent to fetch at the stream, and are looking for gossip. *Nonsense and tenpence!* I turned away to the kitchen in the backyard. I cooked a pottage with a little yam and a lot of the vegetables that grew in the hedge between my compound and Ma'Caro's. I put away my farming gear. I didn't go to farm today.

In the evening I watched the black-and-white TV I inherited from my father. It is almost my age-mate and to keep the pictures from drifting up and down like the thoughts of a mad man, I have to tap it every now and again. That was how I spent the night of my first day away from the farm this year: slapping a thirty-year old television in a mud-hut masquerading as a sandcrete house, watching programmes from the other side of the universe.

I should hate Meme Jumai, if I were not Meme Jumai.

2nd June 2000

ANOTHER SHAMEFUL DAY AWAY FROM my farm. The voice of Nwozuai the gossip woke me up from sleep. He was wheedling *akara* — shameless forty-year-old ne'er-do-well who hasn't done a spot of work in years — from Ma'Caro next door. I stared at my yams for ages. Fourteen days before the village harvest and only two tubers and thirteen inches of yam left at home! Only last week, my harvest wall had two poles strung with yams. Yet, a calamity had occurred, threatening me with a ne'er-do-well's fate. It wasn't burglary and it wasn't death. It was divorce.

Ma'Abel, my wife for twenty-five years, had left me for a vulcaniser at Warri, leaving with most of my yams. She took, she said, ten yams for every son she gave me. Me, I quarrelled with her arithmetic. Three of the sons for whom she claimed compensation died before they started farming. The other two, Abel and Calamatus, often gave me cause to wish them dead as well.

Yet, it wasn't good arithmetic that won Ma'Abel her arguments with me. It was her complete shamelessness. Come and see the crowd her screams pulled on that May 31st! The whole villagers in Ikerre-Oti gathered in that my compound. Her fellow women circled me like vultures. Many men were there as well, but where the women supported Ma'Abel by heaping insults on my head, the men stayed silent, like a lunatic's embarrassed relations.

As the crowd thickened, she had grown more excited, dragging around my loincloth, with me inside, crying that when she married me all she signed for was to be Mrs. Jumai, but instead I had gone and made her Mrs. Suffer-Head.

Yes I'm poor; but I hate disgrace. I had to yield my yams. That very evening, as I sat at the village meeting, pretending that Ma'Abel's desertion didn't bother me at all, Abel took my transistor and electric fan and followed his mother. Calamatus had left weeks earlier on another of his get-rich scams. *Idiots!*

Had that witch left me fifteen years ago, by the next weekend, I swear, I'd have married again. I swear. But, there are certain things that shouldn't happen to a 49-year-old man in whose nostrils the hairs have started to whiten. Especially with today's cost of dowry.

I chewed chewing-stick awhile, wondering whether Meme Jumai had died years ago and forgotten his body in Ikerre by mistake. Then I crept out into the compound to untie the goat. Nwozuai had succeeded. He pretended not to see me as he swallowed his bean cakes, moving his neck like a boa constrictor doing in a rabbit. I squatted in Ma'Abel's kitchen and warmed the leftover pottage in the pot. I ate some of it and returned to my bed, missing my transistor radio badly and studying my remaining yams the way witchdoctors study the position of kola nuts on their divining mats. *Kai!* How could I manage the yams to make them last the two weeks until harvest? The young day matured and aged in front of my eyes. I lay on my clay bed. I sat up, I lay down, and I sat up. That was how I spent this shameful day; without my radio I couldn't shut out the mocking songs of the giggling village girls who changed their route to the stream to pass under my window. *Witches.* In the evening I ate the last of the pottage and shut in the goat.

I didn't leave the gate of my house today either.

With which face will I look at the villagers on the day after *the day after* the day my family left me for a *vulcaniser*? Tomorrow should be better. By tomorrow Chemist's son would have returned from Dubai. And even if he hasn't, a village as useless as Ikerre-Oti should have found fresher gossip for itself. In the evening, I tried to find something worth watching on television. As all the dials were broken, I used my pliers to hunt for a station, but it seemed that all of them had agreed to be idiots today. I slept early.

3rd June 2000

THE FEARFUL BLEATING OF MY goat woke me at 2 am this morning. My useless heart was banging as if it was a mortar for somebody's pounded yam. Goat-thieves have been harassing our village recently; yet, there're two short and cogent reasons why they just shouldn't go near my goat. Firstly, it is my only goat; secondly, it is extremely pregnant. If they wait another month they can steal her without destroying me completely.

Yet if Penis would listen to reason, would they have named him Penis? Besides, it was pitch-dark outside. None of those reasons were sharp or cogent enough for me to risk my life over a goat. So I took my late father's double barrel down from its hiding place in the zinc and aimed at the moon from a crack in the window; I broke that night into pieces. If I can't sleep, why should anyone else? Afterwards, even my goat fell silent. Yet my heart was *knacking* as if I had shot myself. I swear, if by morning that goat is no longer tied to my *onugbu,* I'll take my gun and my last four cartridges to the Village Square and let what happens happen. People should know that the fact of a man's small penis is no reason to take away his wife.

At first light, I went into the yard where the goat was tethered and saw it lying there on the wreckage of my broken bicycle. *Witchcraft and black magic!* Flies from the pit latrine had already filled its open mouth and nostrils. On the inside of one leg were the marks of snakebite. The sight of that dead goat, with its violently pregnant belly, hit me more than my wife's desertion. I hurried into the latrine and in that darkness, allowed the foolish tears to disgrace themselves. I considered the sufferings of my life. *Nonsense and tenpence!* If they were to bury me with all my problems, they would need a very large coffin. It was two months since I last ate meat of any description and here was this little mountain of flesh, for which I had great plans. God has a lot of cases to judge in heaven! Why couldn't the serpent wait another week for my goat to born and then swallow a whole kid if it so desired?

Yet, were the devil to leave wickedness, who else would employ him? I cut up my goat. *Serpents and demons!* If I tell you there were four kids inside that goat you won't believe it. *Four kids!* And if you see all the saliva I swallowed as I cut up that goat! Part of the carcass I buried in the compound, in the evening I dumped the rest down the pit latrine. What has happened has happened and if Reverend Father preaches everything in his mouth, Mass will never finish. It isn't everything that happens that should enter a diary. There're too many idiots that go around, reading other people's diaries.

I went to farm today. Everyone is still looking at me funny-funny, even though Etina, Chemist's son, is back. Anyway, that's their business. I'm not the first man to lose his wife to another man. I won't even be the last. If only she had enough shame to choose a trader or a landlord or something. A *roadside vulcaniser!* And all this nonsense is because I'm poor, nothing more. Will the vulcaniser say he's more handsome than I am? Will he say I was incapable of making sons?

Anyway, by Sunday my clan will be having a meeting on our land case. I don't normally like village meetings, but this one I won't miss. It may be one final opportunity for me to be rich before I die. My clan has been fighting a land case in Warri for the last sixteen years and the lawyer should be coming to brief us on the judgment. If we win, well, I'll just become rich overnight. And the first thing I'll do with my new car is drive to the Vulcaniser and have him check my tyres. Hopefully, Ma'Abel will be there when I pull up.

And I'll drop his tip on the ground when he's through.

4th June 2000

IT WAS STILL DARK WHEN I woke this morning and I remained like a corpse for a long time. I moved my hand in slow motion until it fastened on a broom — which wasn't there by accident. Then I leapt out of bed like a warrior and slammed the head of the broom against the last of my yams. There was a screech, a furious scrabbling and then, silence. I wasn't smiling as I put on the lamp. There was a deep gouge on my yam, but of the rodent that caused it, no evidence. I can't afford to leave the light on but when I went back to bed there was no sleep for me until dawn broke.

I've never studied yams like this before. Two tubers and eight inches of yam. If breakfast wasn't the worst meal for a farmer to skip, I would simply have left for farm. I cut four inches of yam and boiled it. Is it not the scarcity of venison that made deer the delicacy that she is? To think that the day would come when Meme Jumai would boil yam by the inch! I still recall my harvest of March '95. If my yams of '95 were chickens, these tubers of today resemble the eggs they could have laid! Everything's so stingy nowadays, the rains, the soil, — and now, even my kitchen pot! So I boiled the four inches of yam and ate.

What sort of life is this now? I plant a hectare of yam and now I have to tend it on an empty stomach. It is a real shame: A vulcaniser to steal a farmer's wife and yams!

The local government clerk came in as I was leaving for the farm. He wanted his council tax. I told him that money was something my pockets hadn't seen for months and he said that there was a conspiracy in the village because everyone was saying the same thing. I told him that the moon everybody had seen was no more a mirage and he said he wasn't leaving my house till he had his tax in his hand. Therefore I took my sack of implements and told him to look after my house. He told me that he was warning me, that he would seize my yams! I looked at my two tubers and four inches of yam and my chest began to *knack* again.

Poisonous serpents and demons! I told him that if he didn't leave my house before I opened my eyes, anybody who saw the bites on his body would think I owned a dog. He told me that the reason why they nicknamed him 'The Go-Go' was that he never turned back. I told him that he would soon see the difference between the fly that followed the rubbish to the dump and the one that followed the corpse down into the grave. He pulled out a whistle and shook it in my face. He told me that I was playing with arrest and detention, that a single blow on his whistle would bring the police running; but his voice was shaking as well. So I told him I had no quarrel with that, but that he should also whistle for a hearse for the corpse they would meet with me. He shouted that we villagers were idiots, that we won't pay our taxes but will keep complaining that there was no water in the pump and no chalk at the school. But that was all frustration, because he was shouting from outside my house. I told him that the womb of the pauper had many beautiful and stillborn dreams, and that it was better for me to eat my tax than for him and his boss at the local government to eat it. Then I locked my door and went to the farm.

It is the man and his government that are idiots. As if it made any sense to go looking for something in the pocket of someone who was looking for something.

5th June 2000

THERE'S A PLANTAIN SUCKER ALMOST ready to be harvested along the Katai Road, near the farmlands. It's not mine, but then it isn't anyone else's either. It's there, just off a public road. As I pass it today, I gauge it with my eyes. It isn't quite ripe but I can't risk leaving it beyond tomorrow. In this village, I know that ironing starch is hiding a lot of empty stomachs all over the place. But for Ikerre-Oti's monstrous taboos, I would have unearthed a tuber ahead of the harvest feast — but there's no crime more heinous in Ikerre criminology than the eating of the first fruits before the village idols. And there's no talebearer more adept than the green boughs of a yam plant, wilting after the secret rape of its underground tube

The gossips seem to have formed a scandalous new song about me. Whenever I approach they stop singing and start giggling. That's their business, anyhow. Their mates are waxing records and making money, they, they are forging songs with other people's affairs.

Samuel Ekiti came in unexpectedly this evening after I returned from the farm. He surprised me as I was drinking the palm wine I harvested from a tree on my farm. There's a story behind that single palm tree and I'll tell it here. It is the type of tree experienced tapsters call 'The Trap'. It's about forty feet tall with a nick in the middle. The weight of a man on its crown may just be the thing to break its trunk. No experienced tapster would climb a tree like that. Indeed it would take a very desperate boy to try it. Well, yesterday I climbed it under cover of darkness and tied a gourd to its crown. This morning I climbed it just before dawn and brought down my prize.

After all, it's my birthday. If I can't eat like a human being let me at least drink wine like one. When I think of the kind of party that my father must have thrown on the birth of his only son, even the wine is not sweet anymore. Yet, I have to stop thinking all these bad thoughts. Ma Abel used to say that it was bad thinking that made my face squeeze up like an old man's scrotum.

Despite my precautions, Ekiti must have spotted my gourd up the tree. Reluctantly, I share the blood-bought wine with him. In exchange, he offered me some of his snuff, which of course I rejected. The sort of insults one gets in this village. You offer a fellow premium palm wine and he reciprocates with an evil-smelling snuff! So that the day you pay him a visit, unless you catch him at a meal, he won't feel obligated to entertain you!

I spent a lot of time, while Ekiti was sitting there soaking up my wine, thinking about Ma'Abel. All those years I was priding myself that I had chosen well, that I had ended up with a woman who did not look her age. Other men of my age had wives that looked like their mothers; I had a wife that looked like my daughter. I thought I had paid the price of my privilege when I started hearing rumours about Ma'Abel and the councillor, Ma'Abel and the butcher, and Ma'Abel and the owner of the Postal Agency. Then Ma'Abel ran away to the vulcaniser! *Devil, lend me money!* Isn't it better to have a wife that looks like your mother?

I was thinking all those evil thoughts that make a man's inside bitter even when he is drinking sweet palm wine, when the village miser stood up and said he was going. He took my empty cup and sucked it just to make sure. Then at the door, he said to me, Sorry about your goat.

Sorry about my goat! I spent an hour after the sponger left, trying to figure out his words. *Sorry about my goat!* My wife left and he didn't come to commiserate. My sons left and he didn't come. Then my goat dies and he turns up. How did he know about my goat to begin with? There's something about this that I don't like.

6th June 2000

THIS IS MY FORTY-SEVENTH year on the farm and I've never seen a year this bad. There are still nine days until harvest and I don't like the prospects of my kitchen at all. I leave for church without breakfast. I don't know what kind of demon pushed me to do my father's second burial last year. That week of the feast was the last time I had money in my pocket; and it was all borrowed money. Even now I still have Fasmin and Kemberi to pay; and what has made me lose weight like this, if it is not the campaign of insults I have endured over their money. They send their uncouth children to demand their money at the most embarrassing moments. Last week a 7-year-old held my wrapper at a village meeting wailing that his daddy needed his money to pay his school fees.

Although I'm going to church, I carried along a jute bag for the plantain and made a detour through the Katai Road. It's a quiet road on Sundays, perfect for a discreet harvesting. I'm still a hundred metres from the plantain sucker when I realise that a thief has been there already. It's difficult for me to believe what I am seeing. There's so much hunger in the land. People can't even keep their hands from larceny.

I was dizzy with anger and hunger when I reached the church. Warden Isaac must have noticed, because he looked the other way when I stepped over his rope to take a seat at the back, in the place reserved for church elders. I couldn't stay till the end of the service though. Reverend Iwu's sermon was on hypocritical Pharisees as usual. It wasn't more boring than usual, but people kept glancing at me when he uttered his perpetual 'woe unto you's. After a while I couldn't stand it any longer and I just left.

By now, my hunger was as wicked as a demon. I dared not stay at home for fear of eating my remaining yam. I decided to visit Chemist, who is actually my second cousin Nezianya, to rejoice with him over the safe return of his son from Dubai. The crook was out with his entire family. He was clearly trying to get out of serving refreshments to well-wishers. Can I blame him? His son is going to Dubai and back. Mine has gone to the vulcaniser for good.

Because I saw the entire Mentu family in church, I'm afraid I plucked a pumpkin from their house as I passed by their hedge. The whole thing was a conspiracy between my bowlegs and a larcenous machete. I was already bending down before I reached the pumpkin and before I knew what was developing, the pumpkin was in my sack. I felt sorry immediately. But what has happened has happened.

In the afternoon I went for the village meeting. I got there late, to give them time to finish the collection of monthly dues. To avoid unnecessary attention, I also sat at the back. When the time came for the lawyer to talk, he stood up and started some nonsense about 'interlocutory this' and 'exparte that', ending by asking for refresher fees if we were still serious about our case. I left them debating a new family levy. That's the problem with these useless meetings. You can't spend one hour without someone finding a reason to separate you from money you don't even have.

I was thinking about the pumpkin throughout the meeting. In all my adult life, I have never stolen another man's thing. Could hunger change me, or was I a thief all along without knowing it? In the night I cooked the pumpkin with a little yam.

It wasn't even sweet.

7th June 2000

I LEFT FOR THE FARM with only my machete and hoe. Until the day of harvest my farm work will be mostly weeding. Erosion had eaten up most of the Katai Road. The children from Ikerre-Oti Comprehensive jostled with us farmers for right of way on the remainder of the road. They are going to school and they are happy! I that went to school for thirteen years only to lose my wife to an illiterate vulcaniser.

Chentus saw a boa constrictor on his farm. Instead of shouting for help like a well-bred Ikerre-Oti man, he struggled with it like a madman. Greedy idiot. All he did today was roast snake from morning till evening. His shoulder was bleeding from where he fell against an anthill, but he did not seem to mind, so long as he kept the entire boa meat to himself.

The sun slowly roasted my back as bitterness grilled my insides. Was I foolish, twenty years ago, not to have headed for Warri with my school certificate? Yet, Edem had done just that, hadn't he? He had worked twenty-eight years at the Ministry of Works until he was retired three years ago, looking as thin as a palm tree and just as black. All the wretched property he acquired after three decades of office work, didn't they fit into the back of a small pick-up van? After two and a half years of travelling to Warri to pay gratification and push his file, he was told that his gratuity was ready for collection in Lagos. He had learnt idiotic ways in the city too. He threw a foolish party when he got the letter. I still remember the hatred in the eyes of his youngest daughter Eka, as she served rice and the meat they rarely ate at home to the visitors that came to Edem's party. He died in a motor accident on his way back to Ikerre-Oti. A fraudulent Good Samaritan brought his corpse to the Village Square, denying that he saw the gratuity envelope.

I met Nwozuai on the Katai Road this evening. He looked forwards and backwards to make sure we were alone then he brought his melon head close to my ear, so close in fact that I could smell the stale palm wine in his breath.

He told me that what he heard in the market about me was so disgusting that he could never have brought himself to repeat it but for the fact that we were near-kinsmen, and I told him to just say what he had to say and let me go my way.

So he told me how people were saying that hunger had made me eat my decomposing goat.

I told him my goat had died of snake poison and if the rumour was true I'd be dead myself.

He said he thought it was a foolish rumour himself, but that he was repeating it exactly the way he heard it.

As we parted company at the sawmill, Nwozuai didn't know how lucky he was that my machete was in my sack, not my right hand. I knew very well that the next person he met would learn how people were saying that the decomposing corpse that Meme Jumai ate *had even died of snake poison.*

Suddenly, I knew the content of the new mocking songs of the village girls, and the reason for the laughter that kept breaking out behind me everywhere I went in the village. It wasn't on account of my wife and sons. It was on account of my goat. I felt the blood in my head clotting and heating up and couldn't see very well anymore. When Nwozuai disappeared from sight I sat on an old anthill and cursed him for almost an hour. It was fully dark before I found the strength to go home.

8th June 2000

ONE TUBER LEFT AND SEVEN days to go! God will help his own. This afternoon I left the farm early to attend the burial of my distant cousin, Journeyman. For a poor man, it was a well-attended burial, although most people turned out to see the coffin rather than the corpse. Journeyman died last December but because his son was in Rome, our greedy elders refused to bury him. Bury him, bury him, his age grade kept pressing, but no, the elders wanted to eat Italian *lira*. They knew that once Journeyman was inside the ground, it would be impossible to squeeze anything from his son; so they took him to the mortuary and left him there, like kidnappers waiting for a ransom. Imagine that! For five months, a man who died of hunger has been sleeping naked in a corpse's dormitory whose room rate was higher than the biggest hotel in Warri!

It was last week that the elders finally realised that Journeyman's son who had abandoned his father in life had also abandoned him in death. I don't know how they settled the mortuary bill. What I know is that I'm not paying any levy, if they like they can ostracise me, because I didn't join them to scheme for *lira*.

But why am I writing all these things? It's because this afternoon I attended Journeyman's burial. It was a proper poor man's burial. If you want to see people dancing reluctantly then you should attend a pauper's funeral. Today, Journeyman's mourners were dancing purely out of duty, because no one was going to smell food or beer after the dance.

The dead man's body was lying-in-state in Ifetu's casket. Ifetu was another of our cousins. People used to call him a wicked man, but that was a naked lie, because ordinarily wicked people would never have allowed him to enter their meeting-place. In fact, known wizards were careful not to quarrel with Ifetu for fear of haemorrhoids — which were his preferred means of afflicting his enemies. Ifetu knew he had no friends. He also knew Ikerre's penchant for avenging people's misdeeds on their corpses; so he bought himself an expensive coffin, which he stored under his bed. He also dug and plastered a shallow grave right in his courtyard. He figured that whatever grievances his neighbours nursed against him, eventually when his corpse started to stink, someone would tip him into his coffin and push it into the grave.

Unfortunately a drunken truck-driver crushed him last week in far away Ipoti, where he had gone to collect his rents. What was left of his corpse has been festering since then, but the stink of it hasn't disturbed anyone in Ikerre-Oti enough to bring him home to his beautiful coffin. As for Journeyman, kind pauper though he was, nobody was willing to contribute a kobo for his coffin after the lira fiasco. The elders commandeered Ifetu's coffin for his burial; which is how come Journeyman was lying in state in a coffin more expensive than the house he died in.

When I went to see Journeyman's body, I shivered. And I realised why they say that the chick should heed the fate of elder cousins at Christmas, because that will be her fate, come Easter. One look at Journeyman's bony head, and I also realised why they say that it is only what a person eats that he carries to his grave. Journeyman's other children have been peddling the story that their father died of AIDS. What I want to know is: where did Journeyman get AIDS? Do people get AIDS from eating cassava peel? *Nonsense and tenpence!* People just try to win unnecessary sentiments for nothing's sake. Posing with a big man's disease, as if it's hard to recognise the body of a person who died of hunger.

9th June 2000

I LEFT THE FARM THREE hours early today: I lived on fruits throughout yesterday so that I could eat yam today; and when you have tried both you'll notice a difference between blackberries and food. I measured two inches of yam and boiled it with a tray of spinach. My trap had refused to catch bush rats or grasscutters for a few months now so I fried some dried termites to go with the palm oil. That trap of mine is a real puzzle; the last time it caught an animal was the week before Chentus started farming the land between my farm and the river. No matter how early I reach the farm these days, he's there before me. One of these days I'll catch him red-handed. As Ikerre people say, the grains that the chicken spends her life scratching up don't end up in the stomach of the goat.

I was still hungry when I finished my meal so I cracked some palm nuts and chewed their hard kernels, escorting them down with great gulps of water. Every time I cracked a nut I sneezed loud enough to drown the crack of the shell. Ikerre-Oti has the most foolish traditions in the world. There was no child in my house and I couldn't, on top of all my problems, afford the scandal that an old man was cracking kernels like a child.

I tried to sleep but every time I closed my eyes, I saw a host of flies gathering on the red carpet of my dead goat's tongue. Why did I cut portions from the bloody goat anyway? Especially with that evil Nwozuai always dropping in next door to harass his aunt for food. It was desperation, short and simple. And see where the whole thing has landed me now.

I'd buried the goat's entrails and foetuses right away, but I'd also fed Ma'Caro's dog a portion on the sly. The greedy mongrel had never eaten that much meat in its life. I had to drive it from my compound with burning firewood when it wanted to embarrass me.

By evening when I returned from the farm I didn't see it again. It was around six o'clock that I heard Caro wailing. Come and see my chest *knacking!* I allowed one whole hour to pass, then when things quietened a little, I called Caro to the hedge. I asked her after her dog.

It's dead, she told me, beginning to wail again.

I hurried into my house, trembling like a man whose spouse had just tested positive for HIV. That was when I dumped the rest of my goat down the pit latrine. The crying that I cried when I buried my goat was nothing compared with the one I cried when I buried the pieces of my goat.

At least, I didn't cry again when Ma'Caro told me how Johnny Bus-Stop's taxi ran over her daughter's dog. What puzzled her was why the dog was too lazy to dodge a thirty-year-old banger. That exact and particular news, I took like a man. Should I not also have eaten my goat-meat like a man and let what happens, happen? Now, my reputation is in tatters just because of meat that I didn't even taste. This world is not fair at all.

10th June 2000

FIVE DAYS MORE BEFORE the harvest! Unless I start skipping one day between meals I'm clearly going to run out of food. Sleep finished from my eyes at 4 am this morning. I tried and tried but my eyes stood open like a bereaved widow's. I lay there on my bed assessing my last eleven inches of yam. If there's one gift we didn't discuss on the day God made me, it was the gift of fasting. The very thought of a full day without a meal gives me a headache. Particularly when I imagine Ma'Abel cooking my yams for the Vulcaniser.

I am looking face-to-face at Starvation and I have to confess, he's an ugly beast. Yes, Maxwell Otombri seems to be drastically losing weight as well. Even Otudo was recently caught stalking Oba's fowl with his son's catapult. *Shameless man.* Yet, Ikerre-Oti people have been saying it for years, and it's true: the crab in the pot finds no solace in the fact that his whole family is boiling with him.

Kai, but I'm hungry! I dressed for the farm and stole out of my house with some *pirim* seeds in my bag. As early as that, I could hear cackling in Ma'Etibang's darkened house. I'm not surprised that people call her a witch. When I got to my farm I didn't enter, instead I walked down Katai Road, past Chentus' farm, towards the stream. As I neared the trail where I set my trap, I heard that beautiful sound of a crying animal. My heart started pounding again, but this time it had a good reason to do so: there was a bush rat struggling in my trap.

If I can't say the truth in my diary I don't know where else I can say it again. I was just shaking and swallowing saliva as I looked at the rat. It was the fattest rat I have seen in a long time. If you see how its eyes were shining! In the light of my torch, its whiskers were dancing as if it was already roasting on my brazier. A bush rat is a bush rat; but maybe because I hadn't eaten meat in months, it looked as big as a buck. I reached into my bag for a knife to remove its entrails... and my fingers touched the *pirim* seeds.

Kai! There're many kinds of hell, apart from the one waiting for sinners in the grave.

If you saw the fight I fought with myself! I knelt down there in the darkness before my dying breakfast, with my knife in one hand and the *pirim* seeds in the other. Hunger was physically demonstrating to me, what the bushfire did with the ears of the rat, as I tried to decide between my stomach and my head. My stomach was screaming for breakfast but my head was telling me to poison both the rat and the trap-thief. In the end, common sense settled the matter: if I left my house at 4 am again to check my trap people will call me a wizard on top of my troubles. If I wanted to harvest meat from my trap again, I had to solve the problem of the thief once and for all, that very morning.

So I dropped the sweet *pirim* seeds and the rat chewed them immediately. Some animals are cursed. The same long-throat that landed it in soup had now put it into fire. It convulsed and died immediately. I got up and left at once. I've cried over a woman. I've cried over a goat. I'm not going to cry over a rat as well.

I returned home and boiled four out of my eleven inches of yam. By 6.30 a.m. I left for the farm as usual. I checked my trap and it was empty as usual. I started to sing. I didn't think such happiness was possible for a robbery victim.

11th June 2000.

I LEAVE FOR THE FARM before dawn today. I have noticed that a mango tree along the way is slowly ripening its fruit. The disgrace of being seen on a mango tree is something that can drive a fifty-year-old Ikerre-Oti man into exile. The small girls don't even need to coin a song. They have many ready-made ones into which to slot one's name. This is the sort of thing that my sons could have been doing for us had they not succumbed to the temptation of quick money and pumping tyres.

I got to the tree before dawn and I was still up there when Samuel Ekiti arrived underneath. He had already hoisted himself on the lower bough when he heard me rustling in the tree. He paused. Because of that horrible snuff of his, he's the only man I know who snores while he's awake. I could hear the fear in his breathing, which slowly gave way to anger.

I listened to that breathing for a long time, forming the furious conviction that he was same thief who stole my plantain on Sunday. He must have known that I was no snake. Yet, he dared not use his torchlight. To expose me was to expose himself as well, for his feet were also firmly on the mango tree. Eventually, fifteen minutes before it would have been light enough for us to recognise each other anyway; he hurried away, perhaps to find another tree. I contented myself with the dozen fruits I had picked already and hurried off to the farm, with my harvest sack heavy with something more than tools today.

At the farm this morning, I noticed a termite trail that led from a new anthill and I emptied a small bottle of kerosene across the trail and over the hill. There were some beetle holes as well, but since I didn't have money for pesticides, there was really nothing I could do about it.

I don't work very long before I tire. During the worst of the heat I sit in the farm shelter and eat mangoes. All the while I was eating the fruits all I was thinking about was roast bush rat. After throwing away the last of the mango seeds I dried my hands and sighed deeply, all the while looking lustfully at the lush yam bushes on their poles. God knows that I cannot afford another scandal right now; otherwise I'd dig up a yam tuber on the sly, ahead of the village harvest festival.

In the evening I boiled and ate four inches of yam. Then I put on the lace outfit I made for the second burial of my father. I also removed the last three inches of yam from the pole and placed it behind my trunk. Why should any visitor see three inches of yam on fifteen harvest poles? If I am starving, do I have to announce it to the whole world?

I went over to Chentus' house near the butcher's yard. His wife was counting the eggs laid by their chickens. Where's your husband? I asked.

He went to Chemist to buy diarrhoea medicine, she said.

Is that so? I asked sympathetically.

She was still counting her eggs as she confided, Since this afternoon, all of us in the house have been shitting like agric chickens.

But can't you see the wickedness of human beings? They have their chickens at home; they eat eggs every blessed day, but they won't leave my rats alone for me. That's too bad, I told her. Tell him that the next time he takes meat from my trap it will be real poison, not *pirim!* The woman's mouth fell open, giving the game away.

I went home thinking the sacrifice of my rat meat well worth it.

12th June 2000

I REALLY DON'T KNOW HOW I entered Barika's shop on my way from the farm this evening. He was grooming his sleek beard behind his cash register as I walked shamefully around his aisles. It was perhaps the only supermarket in Ikerre-Oti deserving of the name.

Eventually, I approached the richest man in Ikerre-Oti. Behind him, a greying poster advised, *No Credit Today, Try Tomorrow.* He smiled genially at me, Chief Jumai; we haven't seen you for a long time! For Barika, every customer was a chief. It was foolish flattery like this that separated people from their money.

I told him that people did not go on condolence visits with empty hands, and that it was the emptiness of my hands that had kept me away from his shop.

Barika punched his cash register with regard to a stove wick for Edna as he laughed and replied with his own proverb. True, Chief Jumai, but all that's necessary for a condolence visit in respect of a dead goat is a skinning knife.

I paused. The proverb was in standard use, though hardly apt, but my unfortunate connection with dead goats caused me to examine the old trader's face for sly undertones. He smiled, as I realised why Ikerre-Oti people say that in a dwarf's presence, bending down is construed as an insult.

I decided I wasn't in a position to be sensitive. I have come to you in respect of a *little* c-c-c-credit, I said, You know very well that harvest is three days away, and that I planted a few hundred bushes of yam... I couldn't continue, for the mournful look had entered Barika's face. He picked up his calculator and began to punch an idle fortune.

How *little* a credit have you come for? He asked, and I came straight to the point, putting a 2-kg bag of semolina on his checkout counter.

Just for *two* days, I added.

Barika sighed and put away his calculator. You remember that story of Tortoise and Hyena? He asked me.

Which particular one? I asked, disliking the trend of the discussion. I had come for food, not the kind of foolish folktales Abel spent his life spinning instead of farming or looking for a proper job. Yet, if the hearing of a tale was the price of food then I was desperate to pay it.

Hyena was cooking the pottage for which he was famous, began Barika, resting his head on the *No Credit Today* poster. The smell of it was so bewitching that all the animals gathered in envy. Yet it was Tortoise and his sweet tongue that got to eat it all. You've forgotten how? He promised Hyena his beautiful daughter in marriage in return for his pottage! It was an irresistible bargain for Hyena, whose foul breath had made a notorious bachelor. Many months later, when the debt became bad, Lion's court sat and Hyena made his case. You must remember Tortoise's defence: Oh King, Hyena gave me his pottage knowing I had no daughter. I still have none, but when I have one, most certainly, he shall have his bride! And the king said...

Barika broke off his story to punch his cash register in respect of Dumbili's loaves. Several gossips who seemed more interested in Lion's judgement than in their shopping were hanging around, glancing from me to the bag of semolina as the miser in Barika counted and recounted Dumbili's money. I drifted around his shop a little, and when I got near the door, slipped out.

They can have the story.

I headed for my trap only to find a grasscutter struggling there! I didn't know, between my dinner and myself, who was shaking the more. It was the back of my hoe that killed it. I didn't know, between the sweat on its fur and the saliva in my mouth, which was more. I returned home right away. It must have been a small animal, because I ate it once and it was finished. In fact it must have been an *infant* because the only bones left in my pot, from which I ate directly, were claws.

Hunger is a terrible thing. Once I started eating, I just couldn't stop. I that threw in my last three inches of yam, planning to stretch the meal till harvest, I couldn't stop eating until it was all gone. True, hunger is a demon.

Food is good, and anyone who disagrees should just step aside for me.

13th June 2000

AND I THOUGHT I WAS suffering before! Today was the pomp and plain beginning of my nightmare. From morning until 5 pm, the only thing that moved inside my mouth was my tongue. Somehow, I managed to finish my work on the farm. It is still two days to the harvest, yet my pots were as empty as the mind of a simpleton. Sometimes I think that this village is dedicated to the devil. The sorts of wicked traditions that it has! Why can't a man eat his own crops before the collective sacrifice is made at the village harvest festival?

When I returned from the farm, I hobbled over to the bathroom stall like an invalid. Over the hedge, Nwozuai told me that while Calamatus was duping people left, right and centre, my senior son, Abel, was sending emissaries from the Vulcaniser's clan to ask for the hand of an Ubiaja girl in marriage.

Which is another clear evidence that Meme Jumai is actually dead. What else can explain my absence from my first son's marriage? First he hides his girlfriend's pregnancy from me — as though I'm the village wizard whose favourite delicacy is the content of a swelling womb — now this: *emissaries from the vulcaniser's clan!*

After bathing, I discovered a lizard that had crawled into one of my barren pots. It had been dead a couple of days. I threw it away. I saw how it was possible to die the death of a lizard, a death without heritage, lying three or four days in my bed before I am discovered, and even then, thrown away with hissing, with neither outcry nor mourning. I washed my pot grimly. The passing of a man should be different from the passing of a lizard.

I noticed that my house was beginning to dance gently in front of my eyes. I dressed slowly, deciding that it had to be the Etongs, a large, wealthy family of eight sons and not a single daughter. They have a farm more than ten hectares large and their stall at the expressway market is still full of yams and snails to this day. Yet, even though Chief Etong was my distant cousin, and my father once served an apprenticeship in the blacksmith forge of his mother's stepfather, going to their house wasn't an easy decision.

Back in '89 when Calamatus had his appendix operation, Chief Etong had visited us in hospital. To impress the villagers who had gathered at the bedside to commiserate, he rebuked me for not coming to his house to collect his own contribution towards the hospital bills. He reminded me that we were Africans, that one man's problem was his brother's burden. That very night, I was at his house and he said Tomorrow. I was at his house the next day and he said Tomorrow. He said Tomorrow eight more times before I abused him thoroughly and went home.

Yet, wasn't that ten years ago? Since then we have resumed exchanging greetings and sharing kola nuts. I got there just before 6 pm and I stayed two hours. Despite the stunning aroma of Afang soup coming from the kitchen, a callous thing happened. Mrs. Etong didn't bring the family dinner into the parlour as usual. Instead, from 7 pm onwards, the family took turns at disappearing into the kitchen from which they emerged minutes later with a glass of water and a toothpick in the corner of their mouths. Chief Etong himself, with whom I shared a locker in form five, shamelessly made his own disappearance and returned only to fall asleep in front of me.

It was when he started snoring that I went home. — It wasn't me who wrote a desperate letter to Abel. I sat there watching my right hand scribbling the most sycophantic idiocies. I sat there, watching my hunger consume my shame the way dogs lick up vomit. I don't know what miracle has happened to him in two weeks, but if Abel has money to marry his Ubiaja girl, he should have money to feed his own father for two days. I can't sleep much tonight. If I send the letter through Johnny Bus-Stop first thing tomorrow, I could get Abel's cash by evening.

14th June 2000

TOO WEAK TO FARM TODAY. I lay here dreaming of food and listening to voices from the street talking of masquerades and dances for the harvest festival. I reread my letter to my son. It read like something written by a man lying prostrate on the ground. My shame struggled with hunger. I tried to tear the letter but I watched in amazement as my trembling hands folded it away.

At noon I visited my cousin, Chemist. Nezianya eats well, harvest or no harvest. It's just that wickedness has poisoned people's minds; nowadays only those who were formed in the same womb consider themselves to be 'brothers'. If only people will listen to their memories once in a while. Wasn't it just nine years ago that the fake drug scandal blew open and the CID came for Nezianya? Didn't he spend two nights in my pit latrine before someone ate bribe to quench the case? Yet, people are so ungrateful. The last time I mentioned that favour, he had asked me insolently to calculate the two-day rental of my latrine, so he could pay me once and for all.

Anyway, my arrival at Nezianya's house was perfectly timed. The pestle pounding the yam was just tailing off and the heady aroma of *banga* soup was in the air. One of those Ikerre traditions that no one can complain of is this hospitality that mealtimes evoke. Here, it is considered more honourable to skimp on one's children's rations than to deny food to a visitor fortunate enough to walk into a meal. Not only had I walked into a meal, I had met my cousin in a jovial mood, for I heard Nezianya's expansive laughter as I knocked on the door.

The laughter ended as if its owner had fallen inside a river; then a child asked: Who is it?

It's Uncle Jumai, I said. Open the door.

There was some whispering. Then, in a voice apparently strained by a resolve not to have her ration cut in half, the child said: They're not in!

I shook the door handle. It's me, Uncle Jumai, I assured her. I was getting angry myself, I mean, who was this brat telling me that I couldn't enter my brother's house? Open I say, let me message you!

Then something strange happened to the voice. In fact, it was after what happened at Nezianya's door that I accepted that things have utterly spoiled in this country. The voice started out childlike, cracked mid-sentence, and ended up an angry roar: *I say they're not in, what is it? GO AWAY!* I staggered back, shaken by the venom in Chemist's voice.

I stumbled away, burning with shame. My feet were taking me towards the motor park to dispatch my SOS to Abel. It was a good thing, all told, that I ran into Nwozuai on the way. With his previous misdemeanours still very fresh in my mind, I ignored him completely, but as he approached, his melon head turned left and right and I knew he had news for me. There was something irresistible about Nwozuai's gossip, although I had never known him to bring good news.

He brought his mouth so close that I smelled the stale bean pottage in his breath. *Nonsense and tenpence!* This world is an evil place. Here was Nwozuai's mouth smelling of beans, a man who doesn't have a farm, who hasn't done one morning's work in ten years!

If it weren't for the fact that you and I have the same lineage, he began, and I told him I was in haste. So he told me how Abel's marriage bid had ended. The emissaries had been asked if it wasn't true that the groom's family was so poor that they lived on the meat of dead animals and they were driven home in disgrace. I think Nwozuai would have said more, but by that time I had bitten him twice. He set off down Katai Road screaming as if it was a lion and not an ordinary man that he had been talking with.

Afterwards, I stood there like a palm tree whose crown had withered. Inside me was the emptiness of a man who buries two sons in one day; because I didn't need a soothsayer to tell me that I would never see them again. It wasn't me who told my hands to tear up Abel's letter.

MEME

15th June 2000.

HARVEST DAY. IT WAS DAWN and even the dead could feel the excitement in Ikerre-Oti; as for me, I was so weak I could hardly lift a hoe. By nightfall I'd be prosperous again, but first I needed enough strength to harvest yams.

My father had left me four things: the house, the gun, the TV and my surname. That morning, as I pushed my black and white set into a jute bag, I felt as though I were selling my name. At the electrician's house, his wife was busy folding up their mattress, converting their home into a shop while he sat on his high stool, soldering the guts of a small transistor. All around him, on wooden shelves, were various appliances that hardship had pushed their owners to sell. He had cleaned them up now in preparation for harvest and the seasonal prosperity of Ikerre people.

I put my TV on his workbench, not liking how it looked amongst the other TVs in the workshop. It works like new, I told Okosisi, who wasn't a very polite man: You yourself know that they don't make televisions the way they used to.

At first I thought he had seen something funny in the radio he was mending, but when he continued to laugh after it fell and broke, I realized he wasn't going to make me an offer. My heart was doing that nonsense again and my saliva had become a resinous gum. I went home.

The sun had come out well well before shame allowed me to enter Ma'Caro's house. *Please* can I have a plate of pap? I said to her.

It isn't a strange thing to ask for food in a *buka*. But the way I said the *please* warned her that I didn't have the means to pay for it. I had never done that before. I could see that she was frightened I might start weeping in her presence. She hurried into her kitchen for some food. By the time I made the cover of my house, I was actually weeping out of shame.

It was eight o'clock before I was finally ready for the farm. It was just as I stepped out of the house that the first of the villagers returned from the farmlands, leaping and rolling on the ground. They were screaming: *Termites! Beetles!* And the way they were rolling in the sand, you would think the insects were in their pants rather than their yams.

Why people have to be so emotional is what I don't understand. I returned my harvest basket to the house and went to the farm with only my hoe. It was my longest journey ever. I met many more hysterical villagers. I saw many tubers riddled with holes, but I said not a word. It was that resin thing in my mouth again.

Yet, my mind was sparking. *Kai,* but this world is wicked. Is there nothing like fairness anymore? Is there nothing like mercy? Is there nothing like justice? Is there nothing like salary after a hard month's labour? Like harvest after a terrible, terrible planting? The first tuber I dug up was riddled with holes. It had just enough starch to keep the yam plant healthy, not enough to sell, not enough to eat. I didn't dig up another.

The walk back to my house was my shortest, but full of memories. I walked carefully, like a full gourd of palm wine that must not spill. I remembered the day I named my second son. I had written to my father requesting that he send a name. He was in Utagba-Uno at the time, a messenger at the postal agency. So he sent a letter back: Calamatus. I turned the name up and I turned it down. *Calamatus.* So I asked Johnny Bus-Stop, who delivered the letter in his taxi, whether there was a name like Calamatus among the people of Utagba-Uno, and he said that his own business was to bring the letter and not to interpret it. So I named my second son Calamatus. And when people asked me, Calamatus? I told them to keep the question until my father came.

Was that not how, that Christmas, my father visited and asked whether it was a specie of vegetable we were referring to when we spoke the name Calamatus or a human child.

So I asked: Weren't you the one that sent the name?

And he said, No, that *Clement* was the name he told the letter-writer and that the boy *knacked* his head, *knacked* his head, and wrote what he wrote. But by then it was too late. Calamatus had become Calamatus. The tailor had erred in his cutting, and it must become a new style.

I'm home, now. I packed away my tools carefully and lay on my bed. I listened to the voice of the village from morning till evening. It was a bad harvest for yams but beans and cassava farmers were not too badly off.

When I heard the sound of their harvest masquerades whooping on the streets, I rose and brought down the double barrel. It has four more cartridges. It is enough. I will take it to the Village Square and square up with the wicked. My father left me a heritage, and I'll leave my village one. If a man finds no rest for his elbows, he can at least use his knees. I've crawled through life like a lizard but I won't die like one. I am leaving now for the Village Square, and let what happens happen.

DIARY TWO

CALAMATUS JUMAI

Occupation:	Adventurer
Residence:	Porta, Delta State, Nigeria
Date of Birth:	August 19, 1975
Date of Death:	July 6, 2000
Cause of Death:	*Awaiting Inquest.*

17th June 2000

OKAY, I'LL KEEP PA'S DIARY. Let that be my inheritance from him. They looted our compound before turning it into a rubbish dump. Hungry people. Yet, a madman's notebook wasn't the sort of thing they were looking for. When I cleared out the room to sleep, I saw it in the crack between the clay bed and the wall.

This is war!

I've been looking for fame, but not this type. *This is really war!* I went to the Village Square three or four times, but everything was still like cinema... this... roasted animal inside burnt-out tyre wires, is this really Meme Jumai? My father has finally seen what the arrogant soup saw that gave her the complexion of faeces. The villagers were just following me around, jeering. Pa went mad, yes, but the truth is that these Ikerre people are devils. They just phoned me and told me to come, that my father was very sick.

Is he dead? I asked the Igwe of Ikerre-Oti.

Just come, he told me.

Is it stroke? Is it heart attack? Just tell me! There's nothing my ears can hear that will make them bleed.

Just come, he told me.

So I told FazO, who lent me a Mercedes to travel in. He must have known that Pa was dead because he put fifty thousand naira in the boot of the car. *Fifty thousand naira!* This boss of mine! My own millions haven't arrived yet, but anybody that reads Billy Barber's faxes will know that it's not very far away.

So I came, only to find that Pa was dead and the corpse that was left over after the appetite of the fire was quenched wasn't even enough to fill a *ghana-mus'-go* bag, not to talk of a coffin. Abel must have known what happened and allowed me to suffer this shame all by myself, that my brother is a snake. It can't be the disgrace of his failed marriage to that pompous girl that is still vexing him, because all of us suffered it together. After all, the girl is eight months pregnant and has refused to leave him up till now. *He* got something out of it. Me and my friends, we were just disgraced for nothing's sake.

It's only now that Pa has died that I'm beginning to understand him. And is it not this his diary that did it? Pride is a terrible thing, O. This our Pa that will do his face like ironwood and you won't know he's suffering inside. His tongue will be rough like sandpaper. Come near him and his mouth will strike you like cobra. But everything was just for show. See what was inside him: was this not an ordinary human being?

This is war!

Even without reading Pa's diary, if I saw the chance I should have killed Nwozuai and that rat-thief, Chentus, long ago. And that greedy Barika as well. But it is only after reading it that I understood about that Etong. The only corpses Pa made before they lynched him were Etong, Nwozuai and Chentus. Barika's shot caught him in the buttocks, coward. He's still in hospital but I don't think he will die. Why couldn't Pa get more cartridges before starting his *james bond*? After all, who is Nwozuai or Etong and what is Chentus worth that he should die because of them?

I walked round the square many times wondering what to do. This world is very, very wicked. I've been licking the pepper of its wickedness since I was eight days old, when the witch that called herself a midwife sneezed during my circumcision and castrated me. I've been asking for her name since I was twelve years old, but by then my parents had known my mind and refused to tell me. There are more than fifteen nurses in Ikerre old enough to have circumcised me and every time I meet one of them, if only they knew my mind as well!

They burned Pa beside the open gutter. If it rains once, what remains of him will be washed into the sewers. Normally, one needs guts to bury the victim of a lynch mob. Pa's corpse also requires a shovel and a bucket. Yet, I know these Ikerre people. Very soon, they'll be mocking me, saying: Look at him! Shovel and bucket, that's what he used to bury his father! So I went home, cleared the rubbish inside the house outside and went to bed.

But I couldn't sleep. So what will I do when Abel's child grows up and asks for his grandfather's grave? Will I take him to the gutter in the Village Square? Will I take him to the descendants of the village dogs that shared Pa's roasted flesh? There are some things that aren't good for the mouth of a human being to say.

At midnight I returned to the Village Square.

I used a shovel and bucket to collect Pa's remains. The angry dogs I disturbed followed me all the way home. So Pa has become a dog's dinner, eh? It was there, standing at the gate, looking at hungry mongrels licking their mouths and salivating for Meme Jumai, that my eyes leaked a little. There are only two people I want their names: the person who brought the tyre and the person who scratched the matchstick. The rest of the villagers can wait for the judgment of God, but those two will join the midwife that castrated me to experience hell in this world.

This is *war.* Pa was smelling like rotting *suya.* So what do I do with him now? If I quietly dig a grave this night, won't that be the burial of a lizard he was afraid of? I tied him inside a jute *ghana-mus'-go* bag and put him behind the latrine. At least I haven't buried him yet. When I finished, I entered the latrine and vomited up my breakfast. Whether I will be able to eat barbecue again or not, is what I don't know yet. My head is too hot for me to think what to do next. I am just sitting in front of this diary and thinking. I'm really, really thinking.

This is *total war.*

18th June 2000

MY HEAD WAS VERY HOT. But it is cooling down now. When I read what I wrote yesterday, I just shake my head. Let this book not enter the hands of CID or they will charge me for all the people Pa killed. So Pa just crazed like that, eh? What will my friends be saying in Porta! First he's eating dead animals, now he's shooting people like fowls in the Village Square. So what am I going to do now?

The worst thing is that he wasn't even my father. I was still in secondary school when I came to know that Abel and I were only half-brothers. (This Ikerre-Oti is a small place.) My real father was Ndep Kedu, the owner of the postal agency. If Kedu wasn't such a snake, there were times that I quarrelled with Pa that I would have gone to him. Our useless mother wanted to sleep around and she couldn't even look for human beings. And see what she has done to Pa! If she doesn't suffer before she dies then I am not a bastard. She thinks I'm Abel.

My head is cooling down now. Yet, when I read the things that Pa wrote, it begins to charge again. That man suffered! And it served him right too! If I knew it was like that would I not have helped him? Calling me conman, conman all the time, who is the pumpkin-thief now? — And which is worse: to con money from rich people or to take a double barrel to the Village Square and craze just like that? And why should a poor man be proud like a king? And why should a starving man be doing like he has money in the bank?

This our compound is very large. I will end my apprenticeship with FazO; after all, Billy Barber can't dally-dilly forever. If I leave Ikerre-Oti now they'll never stop laughing at us. I have to show this village that 'Jumai' isn't another name for poverty. Pa should have been more patient: if Billy Barber doesn't enter my trap in another two weeks, then I'm a dog. We would have dealt with these villagers.

But look at this disgrace now!

By 2 pm, the man from the telephone company arrived. I bought him a soft drink from Ma'Caro's house. He asked whether I was Calamatus Jumai and I agreed. He said he had come to survey the place. I told him that what I applied for were telephones, not surveys.

He looked around. Despite the Mercedes I parked outside, anyone could see that Meme Jumai's house had a faithful pet whose name was Poverty. He crossed his legs. He said that the matter of telephone was a very complex one; that after the survey, they would do the assessment and if the report was good, the Exchange Manager might approve it; and if he did, the Territorial Manager might ratify it; and if he did, they would put paper for requisition, and if the materials were in stock, they would apply for operational vehicle and if the vehicle had fuel and the driver wasn't sick, and they could mobilize all their installation team, then I could get the telephones.

I asked how long all this would take and he wrinkled his face and said nineteen to twenty months — if the rainy season wasn't too wet, and the union didn't resume their strike.

So I put fifteen thousand naira beside him and asked, beg pardon?

He began to swallow his Adam's apple. Finally he said he would come tomorrow to confirm whether my 'kola' would push my file up to the table of the Exchange Manager. I calculated a little, and then I added five thousand naira to the money on the table.

(Money is useful when you don't want to talk too much.)

By this time I could hear him drinking saliva. His hands were washing themselves in sweat. He asked if I had the telephone boxes at home. I said I did and he said he would do the internal wiring immediately and phone me tomorrow to make sure that both the new telephone line and the one I was transferring from Porta were working properly.

This is war.

I visited Ugbaja the building contractor. The old man was in a good line of business and would have been richer than Barika himself, except that he married all his girlfriends. As it was, he had the largest family in Ikerre-Oti, counting the Igwe's. He had to run very, very fast, just to stand in one place. He didn't offer me a chair and he laughed when he heard the reason for my visit. He said he didn't know how I got the car but that the money I used to hire a Mercedes wasn't the type of money they use to build houses; that a man should first of all buy land before he begins to talk of building a house.

I told him there was plenty of land in my father's compound and he laughed again and said I would soon understand. So I went home.

In the evening, the smell of the rubbish in the compound drove me to Ma'Caro's *buka*. At first I had been dodging Ma'Caro, thinking she would be vexing because Pa had shot her nephew, Nwozuai. This morning she surprised me and grabbed my jacket across the hedge. I thought she was going to machete me, but she only whispered that although she couldn't be seen to rejoice at her relation's death, Pa's other sins were likely to be forgiven him because he had also removed Nwozuai, the curse of her life, from this world.

Ma'Caro wasn't there in the evening, but her serving girl left her girl friends and brought me a Coke. I touched it. It was warm like piss. I told her to look for a cold one in the ice-chest and she hissed like a snake before asking who gave me the mouth to ask for cold bottle when the whole of Ikerre knew that there was no fridge in my father's house.

As she returned to Ma'Caro's old fridge she was telling her friends that the only problem with giving a monkey cutlery was that before you know it, it will be asking for napkin for its mouth. And if you see the teeth of the girl talking like this, their shape and colour was that of a pickaxe. It's because of this kind of tongue that some girls can never find husbands, even after chimpanzees are allowed to marry human beings. Just one slap would have sent her to hospital. Yet, if I touch her now, nobody will remember how her mouth was stinking like a pit latrine. All they'll be saying is that another Jumai has gone mad again. Instead of getting me a colder bottle, she rejoined her friends and they started singing proverbs on my head. I saw what Pa had suffered.

I vexed and drove to Warri.

After all, my name is Calamatus Jumai, not Meme Jumai.

I bought a brand-new fridge, the first fridge to enter Ikerre-Oti inside a carton. All the other fridges had worked to retirement age in another man's country before coming to do cupboard-work in Ikerre. I drove slowly around the village with the fridge hanging out of the boot, until my vex cooled enough to allow me to go home. By then everybody in Ikerre-Oti knew that Calamatus Jumai had bought a brand-new fridge.

Yes. People started coming to my house to talk about this and that but really to touch my fridge. In two days, my fifty thousand naira had come down to fifteen thousand but when I see the respect in the eyes of the villagers now, I don't mind at all.

Yet, by the time I got home, some jealous people had dumped fresh rubbish in my compound. I vexed again. I wanted to do what gave me the nickname 'Calamity', but everyone was watching me. Pa used to say that a man with madness in his family line should be careful how he laughs in public, before people move away and say: aha, his own has started. So I held myself and sent a message to the Igwe's council that I had a case to bring to them the next day.

19th June 2000

MY HEAD WAS VERY HOT, but it's better now. It's cooling down now. This diary is a good thing. When you are doing something, you may think you're doing something really good. But in the night when you sit down and write it down, you just shake your head and call yourself *mugu*.

Today I behaved as if my head contains corned-beef instead of brains. Today was the meeting at the Igwe's palace. This was how I started the discussion: gently, gently, as if I was a seminary student. All I told them was that I didn't like what they had done to my father's house. All I asked them was why they made my compound a garbage dump, whether they would like it if I turned their own compounds into burial grounds.

And they said I was threatening to kill them!

I asked them when I threatened to kill anybody.

They asked me how else I could make their compound a cemetery if it wasn't by killing and burying them there.

I told them that only fools and dunces could interpret my words like that, after all, I could make their compounds a burial ground for dogs.

That was when the meeting scattered. They all stood up and started spraying themselves with spittle, shouting at the same time, like lunatics, that I was also calling them fools and dunces and dogs, that I have no respect or common sense or home training. Finally after more than one hour they settled the matter by fining me *one* fowl.

Hungry people.

Then and there I should have gone back, not so? I should have gone back to Porta and continued my apprenticeship to FazO in the business that once gave him money to buy five houses in one day. After all, what is the worth of one dirty piece of land in Ikerre-Oti that has no running water or common coal tar road? But there's something that just boiled my blood when I looked at those elders with their brown and crooked teeth, and their brown and bloody eyes, looking at me as if I was already becoming crazy myself, whereas, if you add all the money in all their pockets together it can't be more than one thousand naira.

So I vexed very well and went and bought five fowls from Mama Calabash. (You see, when you have fifteen thousand naira in your boot and one fowl is just three hundred and fifty naira, there is a way that the money can push you and there is nothing you can do. True.) Mama Calabash tied all their legs together and with my vex, I was just dragging them on the ground and going. The fowls were crying and flying and fighting as if the Nigerian Civil War was starting again and by the time I reached the elder's meeting place, chicken feathers were flying all over the place and more than thirty villagers looking for gossip were following me.

When they saw the number of fowls I was bringing, the elders showed me all their brown and crooked teeth. They were smiling as if it was a naked woman that I was escorting inside and not ordinary fowls. Many of them stood up to carry the fowls so I told them that if they liked, all of them could stand up because of fowl, but that so far, their fine was *only* one fowl; that I had brought the rest because of what was still inside my mouth — and the sun was too hot for me to be going up and down to Mama Calabash's shop every time they fined me.

That was when their eyes cleared and they started talking to me with respect. They said it wasn't good for elders to curse their own son, and that the way I was going, that might just happen. They said I should come back tomorrow to allow everybody's annoyance to cool down. They said that it wasn't only through fines that elders should eat the fowls of young men; that there was nothing wrong with me giving them a freewill gift, and that when I was coming tomorrow I should look for an experienced elder to be my mouth.

And, *mugu* like me, I left!

I'm a cow! A *mugu*! Corned beef has blocked my head! I that should have abused them very well, warned them, and ended the matter then and there!

Instead, by the time I returned to the house, more people had dumped their rubbish in the compound. It's jealousy, pure and simple: because of the cable that the telephone company is drawing to my house. Who do they think they are, anyway, to dump garbage in my father's compound just because he killed three people who weren't even real human beings to start with? They're lucky, that's all. If it were me, I'd have killed all of them.

The car, the fridge and the telephone; those are the things vexing them. They're jealous that a man that left Ikerre on two legs how many weeks ago, should return on four wheels. They haven't seen anything yet. Just let Billy Barber swallow my hook.

20th June 2000.

IT WAS THE TELEPHONE THAT woke me up this morning. It was ringing *inside* the house! The phone man came after that and I gave him more money to make sure that the name and address on their phone record wasn't mine.

I connected the fax machine to the transferred telephone line and brought out my telephone books from the car. The first fax I sent was to my fish, Billy Barber, and then I phoned FazO. After that, I drove to the Igwe's house — why he calls it a palace is what I don't know, this place that resembles a mechanic's yard. The palace was fuller than yesterday. The Etong boys are spreading the rumour that it was armed robbery that gave me money to buy a car in how many weeks. Most of the people who were there have come to see Calamatus the Armed Robber.

The Igwe's council asked me what was inside my mouth.

I told them it was still the same thing that was there yesterday; that I wanted Ikerre-Oti to stop dumping refuse on my land, before more bad things happened in the village.

They said it seemed that the snake's offspring was growing a forked tongue as well; that I was sounding more like Meme everyday. They reminded me that they had advised me to hire a seasoned elder to speak for me.

I told them that the best mouth to describe a stomachache was the mouth that owns the stomachache; that I knew what was inside my mouth, and that to save everybody's time, they should take my four fowls and accept everything else that came out of my mouth the way they heard it.

They said I was beginning to insult them.

I told them that that was the whole point.

All that was pretence anyway, because they had already taken the fowls. That's how we started to talk. The Igwe told me I couldn't complain about what the villagers were doing on Meme Jumai's land since it wasn't mine.

I reminded him that according to Ikerre custom, a dead man kept six-by-two feet of his land and left the rest to his sons.

He said that was true, but that according to a superior Ikerre tradition, nobody could inherit a dead person's property until he had buried the person.

I told them to give me Meme's corpse and I would bury him.

They told me that a burial was a very spiritual thing and the absence of a body has never prevented an Ikerre burial. They said that even Esua who was eaten by crocodiles right down to his shoe laces still got his burial; that what was required was the fifteen cartons of beer for the elders, five bottles of Schnapps, three gourds of *kokori* and six thousand naira in lieu of the burial feast.

I told them that that didn't sound very spiritual to my own ears. I asked them whether they wanted to do to me what they couldn't do to Journeyman's son and they said I had insulted them; and that that was one fowl. I asked them if ten thousand naira would satisfactorily bury my father into their stomachs.

Some were shouting, Yes! Yes! Others were shouting, Second fowl! Second fowl! So I opened my boot, brought out ten thousand naira, and threw the bundles on the ground in front of the Igwe.

The insult crazed them, they screamed, Third fowl! Third fowl! But as they were screaming, they were struggling for the money.

Hungry people.

So I asked them whether, now that I had buried my father to their satisfaction, I could inherit his land. That was when I realised why the village vultures prefer the leaking roof of the Igwe's palace for a perch: they have relations inside. The elders scratched their heads as they looked for proverbs to twist into the situation. You see, the Igwe began; this matter of yours is very complex. The firewood you brought us was full of ants...

Why didn't you see the ants before my money came out? I asked them.

It's only when firewood enters fire that ants come out, said the Igwe; it is a very, very complex matter.

I asked them what kind of ants they had found in my firewood.

He said the Ikerre-Oti tradition in question was very serious; (which was very funny, because nobody has ever gone to prison for breaking tradition. They think I'm Meme Jumai who starved himself because of a stupid taboo). He said that by tradition, when a man commits abomination as my father did, his property was forfeited to the village. He said that even if I buried my father twenty times, the land now belonged to the villagers, whose most pressing need was for a garbage dump.

I asked when this tradition began and they pointed at the *iroko* in the middle of Ikerre, and explained that when the seed that became the tree was still in the stomach of the fruit bat that excreted it, the tradition was already a very old one. That was nonsense of course, because everybody knew that sixty years ago, Ikerre-Oti was called Trailer-Junction and its culture was picked and mixed from the five or six major tribes that formed the mongrel town.

So I asked them if it was no longer an abomination for a man to sleep with his own daughter and they screamed that that was the great-grandfather of all abominations. So I told them that if they didn't know, I could point out an elder amongst them who was the product of such a union, who was still living in his father — or grandfather's — house, which was better located for a rubbish dump than Meme Jumai's land.

The Igwe grumbled that it was not necessary to point, but that each case was treated on its own merit.

This is *war.*

I asked them again whether it was no longer an abomination for an Ikerre-Oti man to sodomize a goat and the shameless elder whose son was caught in that disgraceful act jumped up, screaming that we should stop all this digressing about and talk what we came to talk and go home.

So I went to the boot of the car. I wasn't a gourd of palm wine; yet, the hungry villagers followed me like flies. This time, what I brought out was a machete. After all it isn't every time a hen squats that it lays an egg. As I entered the noisy room, all the shouting stopped — it only remained for the cowards to enter the walls. I dropped the machete on the floor and they began to breathe again. I told them I had something to say, and this time they listened.

I told them that Ikerre-Oti people should look for another garbage dump or discover why they nicknamed me Calamity; that if anybody was an abomination, it was the Ikerre people themselves who allowed hunger to drive their brother Meme Jumai mad. I told them that from what I had learnt, the three corpses in the Village Square could have been avoided by three square meals, which was too much to squeeze out of the people of Ikerre-Oti. I told them that any person who still wanted to bring rubbish to my house was welcome to do that, but he should first go around the village to collect messages to our ancestors, because I, Calamity, would send him where I sent the Fulani herdsman.

The Igwe coughed many times but when he started to talk, the voice that we heard was still not his normal one. He told me to remember what happened to my father who was killed in a way that people didn't kill animals; that one man couldn't fight a village; that my father managed to kill three people, but where was he now?

I told them I wasn't fighting the village and that the youths were on my side — after all I was going to build a storey building on my father's land and it was Ikerre people who would get the contracts.

When I said that, despite the machete on the ground, the elders were laughing and falling down. One of them cleaned his eyes and said that burying somebody with ten thousand naira wasn't the same as building a house — unless it was the kind of mud house my grandfather built.

The laughter started again. The Igwe said that in any case no villager would follow me for fear of being ostracized.

Is that so? I asked him.

That is so. He told me, picking up the fan he had knocked to the ground in his laughter.

This is *war.*

I looked around. The place was now so full that if you threw sand in the air, one grain wouldn't reach the ground. Follow me, I said. I turned around and went to my car. When I opened the boot, young boys were crowding me. I put my hand inside the carton FazO gave me and I grabbed everything inside it with my two hands. I didn't count it, but if it was less than five thousand naira, call me a gorilla.

When I raised my hands, my stomach was doing like a cement mixer, because apart from what was in my hand, all the money I had left in this world might not even reach hundred naira. Yet, I threw it into the air — and the kind of shout that they shouted brought everybody in Ikerre running. Before I closed my boot, every currency note had been plucked from the air. Not even one reached the ground, I swear.

Some people were still fighting over torn pieces as the rest of them carried me on their shoulders back into the meeting room of the Igwe's palace. The only thing to hear in the whole village was *Ca-la-mi-ty! Ca-la-mi-ty!* And these were the same idiots who killed my father how many days ago. Yet, if you see what that chanting did to me! If there had been another carton of money in my car I would have opened it, by God!

The elders were silent as I picked up my machete. I told them that I had finished saying what was inside my mouth — but that if there were any fowls left over, they could keep them. Then I went home.

As I was going, my eyes began to clear. Money is worse than

alcohol, true. The cement mixer inside my stomach was vibrating so much that the car was moving from one side of the road to the other. I was just shaking, calling myself cow, *nama, mugu.* In how many days I had burned more money than my father spent in his whole life! I didn't have money to replace the soft drinks in my brand new fridge. I didn't even have enough petrol to escape to Porta. Is this family cursed or what? In the night, I dreamt that a lizard the size of a man was sleeping on Pa's old clay bed. I went to drive it out of the house and it sat up and shouted, in Pa's sandpaper voice: Don't you know me? I'm your partner Billy Barber!

21st June 2000.

I COULDN'T RECOGNISE THE COMPOUND when I woke up. Several young boys had come to move all the garbage out of the house. Yesterday night, the place was a mess; today everything whose father's name was rubbish had disappeared. Pa was lucky that I woke up when I did, because as I came out I saw a jute bag on a wheelbarrow heading for the rubbish dump. That was how I saved Meme Jumai the second time. I carried the *ghana-mus'-go* back behind the latrine.

I didn't talk plenty. I just walked around the compound, nodding my head. I didn't thank anybody. Did I beg them? I just told one of them to fetch water for me to bathe. Then I entered the house again.

Since they were sure I had woken up they came inside to clean the house as well. That was when I shouted at them. I asked them whether they had no home training, whether they couldn't wait till I left the room. They said sorry and ran outside. It was better for me to be very angry, because I didn't have any money to give anybody.

I knew that I was in a terrible soup. I got out my file and began to draft another letter to Billy Barber, but it is very hard to concentrate when there's no money in your pocket.

In the evening, a very bad thing happened. That was how I knew that what was inside these villagers wasn't ordinary envy.

It was a demonised type. I went to stretch my legs, and by the time I came back, the borrowed Mercedes was burning! *Heew!* The fire was blazing and people were just running around and shouting, throwing sand and dirty water into the fire like apprentice cooks adding salt and condiments in soup.

I just stood there like a *mugu,* watching fire consume the thing that separated me from the useless villagers. People surrounded me, saying: Sorry, Sorry, as if it wasn't one of them that scratched the matchstick in the first place.

In the night, Chief Ato and Elder Koiki came in. I gave them Coke. It was so cold that they were sipping it like gin. They said that my fridge was very nice.

I said Thank you.

They said that the compound was very clean.

I said Thank you.

They said sorry about the car.

I said Thank you.

They said that Meme Jumai — may he rest in peace — was a very nice man.

To that one, I couldn't say anything at all. They continued to talk about everything in Ikerre-Oti except what brought them, which was that their dignity had not permitted them to struggle for the money I sprayed from my boot at the palace.

It was very interesting because, after the Igwe, these were the most influential people in the whole of Ikerre-Oti. They had never entered our compound throughout Pa's lifetime. Chief Ato was a popular speaker at traditional feasts and marriages; Elder Koiki was the Igwe's deputy on his council. And yet here they were in my house, giggling like small girls looking for money to perm their hair. Money is a wonderful thing.

At last they stood up to go and I put my hand in my empty pocket and hissed. I told them that the fire had consumed all the cash I had outside the bank, and that next time they came I would find something for them.

They said they understood and promised that anything else I wanted in the village I should just tell them and they would be my mouth and my ears.

I said Thank you.

Just before I fell asleep, another Nicodemus came. This time it was Ugbaja. He brought a carton of wine to 'greet' me and as he unrolled some ancient building plans on the floor, he was sweating and laughing like a fool. I knew that the story of my visit to the palace had reached his ears. About that house... he said.

Which house? I asked him.

That house you wanted to build, he said.

So I told him that I had no plans to build a house. I asked him whether it was because he heard that I sprayed money from a carton that he assumed that the next thing was for me to build a house. I told him that the kind of money that they use to spray villagers was different from the type they use to build a storey building. That was enough insult to craze a normal person, but I didn't know Ugbaja. He began to beg and prostrate. After thirty minutes I couldn't stand the embarrassment anymore and I hired him.

They left me alone after that, but is there any sleep for the stupid? After searching all my pockets, all I found was fifty-five naira. This is the kind of soup into which the son of Meme Jumai has put himself. I'm starting a new building tomorrow. The villagers are waiting for me to vex and replace the burnt Mercedes the way I vexed and bought a fridge. Already poison tongues are bringing proverbs left and right. Meanwhile, all I have in my pocket and my fridge is fifty-five naira and three bottles of Coke. This is worse than foolishness. This must be witchcraft: there must be a curse on the Jumai lineage. In four days I have gone from Mercedes-owner to pedestrian-without-bus fare!

Many times in the night, I stood up, ready to escape to Porta; but it is better for me to hang myself inside this house than to beg an Ikerre-man for bus fare. Throughout this night, all I was thinking was Billy Barber, Billy Barber, Billy Barber.

22nd June 2000

IT WAS IN THE MIDDLE of the night that born this morning that my fax machine began to sing. I read the papers falling like white ash to the ground, then I switched off the light and began to dance in the darkness. I say I began to dance! There was no music but I was dancing with my head and my buttocks and my stomach. It wasn't enough. I lay down and danced but it wasn't enough. It was this morning that I saw with my very eyes the demons of money. And it almost crazed me. Quickly, I opened Ugbaja's carton of wine and poured everything inside one bucket. I took it to the bathroom and bathed. I say I bathed with a bucket of wine! When I finished I was smelling like the belching of a drunkard, but for the first time I could sit down without shaking.

There're demons inside money, true. That's why, all those things rich people do, you can't blame them. As I'm sitting now, I'm feeling like fifteen human beings put together.

I read the fax again. Billy Barber has finally swallowed my hook! After how many months of dallying and dillying, he has finally eaten the hook. This is what the *mugu* said.

> *My dear Dr. Amechi,*
>
> *I've had a good think on your proposal, I must say there were a hundred and seventy million excellent reasons for me to go ahead but I had to deal with the possibility of*

another unexpected expense further down the line. I'm sure you see what I mean. When we started this business, you assured me it was an in-and-out transaction and that nothing was expected of me beyond the provision of a bank account. Since your first letter in April however, I've had to set up a dummy company and pay for a dummy auditor's report. Now after all that expense, you are asking me to cover your Reserve Bank's humongous one percent charge.

However, in view of the substantial sum I've already invested in this enterprise — not to mention my projections for my own share of the money — I've decided, against my personal principles, to defray your Reserve Bank's vetting charge. I've wired the $170,000 into your nominated account. Please confirm my understanding that the $170 million will be lodged in my account latest by the 24th of June. That will enable me to meet my overdraft and other obligations. I trust that there'll be no other delays (and definitely no other unexpected expenses!)

Yours truly, Billy Barber.

One hundred and seventy thousand dollars. I multiplied it into naira and subtracted the commission of FazO's agent in Rajan Community Bank. I began to shake again. I grabbed a bedsheet and ran into the street. Anything that called itself a human being was sleeping. I ran until I couldn't see houses anymore, and everywhere I looked was darkness and bushes; that was when I stopped and began to laugh. I laughed so much that I began to cry and then I cried so much that I began to laugh. When I returned to the house I was so tired that I slept till 12 noon.

The noise of Ugbaja's labourers woke me up. I read the fax again. It wasn't a dream.

I was a millionaire many times over.

I had a proper bath. Yesterday, I had selected one of the youths, Egbuna, to be my houseboy but this Ikerre is a wicked place. They beat him so much on his way home. To reduce the jealousy — and because of the wickedness of these people,

I selected eight more boys. I called six of them bodyguards and I put four of them to guard the house while two of them escorted me in Johnny Bus-Stop's taxi to Warri. The Mercedes they burned down was twelve years old. I replaced it with a brand new one. I entered Ikerre by 4 o'clock. For the next two hours I was driving around the village. By the time I finally parked the car, there was no street in the village that didn't carry the tyre mark of my new car. Even the blind of Ikerre had learnt that Calamatus Jumai had replaced his burnt car within twenty-four hours.

Yet, when I finally parked the car, if I say I wasn't afraid, I will be lying. The wickedness of these Ikerre people has begun to fly in the afternoon. The jealousy on their faces! When they look at my new car, I can see a terrible pain on their faces: it is as if my new car is a knife twisting inside their stomachs! I can see now why rich men who live among paupers are always suffering headaches. Quickly, I put two bodyguards on the car to watch it day and night. If these people's eyes were matchsticks, me and my car would be burning by now.

Even my bodyguards are a big problem. By evening, they had washed the new car three times. Every time I drive in they attack the car with detergent and buckets of water. If I didn't slap them the last time, by tomorrow the red car would have become pink.

Johnny Bus-Stop's son came to see me today. He wanted to be my driver. Among his age mates in Ikerre-Oti, he was the best driver. I looked at him. His nickname is Nacet, because of the penknife he carries everywhere, yet, if you see this person, he has the body and the voice of a small girl. After his only fight in this village, they beat him so much that he ended up in the health centre. He didn't look like the kind of person that should be driving Calamity. I asked him if he hadn't heard the rumour that I was an armed robber, and he said that if I liked, I could be a kidnapper and ritual killer, he still wanted to be my driver.

I hired him immediately.

Late in the night, as I was sending my faxes, I heard shouting in the compound. When I came out, I saw that my houseboys were about to kill Etong's first son. He had been caught by my boys secretly dumping a basket of rubbish in the compound.

By the time I reached them, Uti Etong was already naked. They had beaten red into his eyes and flogged blood out of his body. *This* is *war.* I saw Nacet running into my compound with a tyre and I told them to wait. I didn't say anything until they brought a chair for me.

Many things passed through my head as I sat there looking at Uti, who was two years my senior in secondary school. Now, he was breathing like a fish pulled out of water. His eyes had that fear of a sinner queuing at Heaven's gate without a visa. I knew that Uti could die that minute without my lifting a finger; — after all, didn't I warn the Igwe-in-Council? Yet, his death could easily become the bone that choked the greedy man to death.

It was as I sat there before a dying Uti that I knew that *talking* about killing, and *killing* were two different countries entirely.

What most people have forgotten by now is that before I got the nickname Calamity, they used to call me *Wee-Wee* because of the day I wet myself at assembly while the headmaster was flogging me for something I can't even remember. Abel and I were on the way to school one harmattan morning when we found the corpse of a nomadic Fulani cattle herdsman. He had died there overnight and his flock of ten white cows was standing around him like a football team waiting for their captain to recover from injury. The man's body had all the wicked charms and daggers that made Ikerre people fear herdsmen; but when death came, they didn't save him.

Abel and I argued over who killed the nomad for some minutes, but Abel's intelligence had given him the nickname, Booker T, so my case was more urgent. He ran back to Ikerre, screaming that a mad Fulani warrior had attacked his kid brother. By the time the first villagers arrived, armed with guns and sticks, I had rolled myself in mud and blood, torn my own clothes, and stuck the dead man's knife into his chest. They were standing there speechless, staring at me as I lay panting beside the cattleman and his silent animals. When Abel hailed me 'Ca-Ia-mi-ty!' They all joined him; and that was the end of my former nickname.

Between Uti Etong and the boys trying to kill him, I didn't know whom I hated more. In the morning the boys would have disappeared — as they all did after the killing of Meme Jumai. It was inside my house that Uti's corpse would be lying. Eventually, I asked them, Where's his trouser?

My boys looked at me as if I was crazy, Nacet raised his tyre. Did you say *tyre* or trouser?

You want him to piss on me? I yelled. His own clothes were in pieces, so they found him a pair of old knickers from the rubbish outside. This life is very interesting. As soon as the short knickers covered the boy's nakedness, as soon as the gates of Heaven and the heat of hell faded away, Uti's shoulders started to curve with that arrogance that marked out the Etongs in this village. By the time he finished buttoning the knickers he was behaving like someone who was two years my senior in school. I knew that by tomorrow the story of how Uti Etong defeated Calamity's thugs would be circulating in the village.

That was when I knew what I was going to do. There's only one punishment for robbers. I told him, but you're a young man and I'll give you another chance. You see that barrow?

He said he had seen it. Get on your knees. I told him. When he had done that, they filled the wheelbarrow with garbage, tied it to him like a donkey and my boys escorted him home, singing the mocking songs for apprehended thieves. If it is sweet like this to assassinate a person's character, why did they burn Meme Jumai?

I returned to my fax machine and sent faxes for the next three hours before I fell asleep. As I slept, I dreamt that I went to eat in a *buka* whose waiter was a monitor lizard. He wore a plastic apron and asked, in a sarcastic voice that was rough like sandpaper, whether I wanted to eat meme barbecue or meme peppersoup.

23rd June 2000.

I COULDN'T FORGET THE DREAM all morning. I read what Pa wrote only ten days ago. I can't just leave a roasted human being in a bag behind a latrine, that's true. Yet, wasn't he the one that said he didn't want a lizard's burial? If I dig a grave at night and put him inside, isn't that the very lizard's burial he was afraid of? And what's the point of holding a proper burial feast that nobody — including his first son and his wife will attend? I was just hissing and thinking about this problem when Egbuna, one of my houseboys, came and began to polish my fridge. There's something I want to tell you Sir, he said.

What? I asked.

In the village, people are saying that you can't be an armed robber.

I laughed and asked, Why is that?

They say that if you're an armed robber, your victims are not in this country. They say a flea can never be fatter than his dog.

I see, so what have they decided that I am? A ritual killer?

Egbuna was silent for a long time: No Sir, they say that you're either a 419 conman, or a cocaine dealer.

I laughed again, And what makes them think so?

The way you spend money without counting it, he said. Ordinary people go to bank with envelope, you go to bank with cartons.

So I explained to him that I was a *con-artist,* not just an ordinary conman, and that anyone who thought it was easy to tell lies and get rich was welcome to try it. After all, there's no Chartered Institute of Fraud signing only fifty certificates a year to keep their members rich. It wasn't like medicine where they take seven years worth of examinations for the right to wear stethoscopes. I told him that human beings could puke if they wanted, but that as far as the bitch that ate her puppies after eating her placenta was concerned, she was very, very hungry.

He told me he was very hungry himself, that he had no quarrel with dogs eating dogs and that in fact, he wanted to be my apprentice in the business. So I told him to bring a knife that didn't have any wood in it.

Egbuna was away for a very long time. When he came back he closed the door and stood there shaking with the knife that didn't have any wood in it. I told him I had two questions for him. He just stood there shaking. I asked him if he brought a tyre for my father and he said 'no'. I asked him if he scratched the matchstick that burnt my father and he said 'no'. I told him I wasn't forcing him to do anything, and he said he wanted to; so I told him to say what he had to say concerning my life and my property.

So he begged the knife and all the relatives of the metal in the knife to do the most terrible things to him and his children's children should he ever plan evil against my life and my property.

When he finished I was satisfied, but ten minutes after he left, the other boys came in with knifes that didn't have any wood in them.

I went to Warri. I must tell the truth, life is sweet. At my bank I loaded the boot with money and drove to a car lot where I bought another Mercedes. I returned to the bank where I loaded the new car with money as well. I stopped at a store and bought typewriters and fax machines, then I drove to the main market where I loaded some tippers with building materials. We returned to Ikerre-Oti in a convoy of vehicles.

I think that will give the hungry people of Ikerre-Oti plenty of gossip for a long time.

I sent my houseboys to the market and told them to cause a scarcity of meat there.

They asked what I meant.

I told them to buy all the meat in the market for my father's burial. Only Egbuna had the courage to be a rich man's servant. The others have too much poverty in their blood. He left for the market without waiting for money. The others were still asking how many people I was expecting and arguing that the meat would spoil, when Egbuna returned. He wasn't even carrying any meat. He had told the butchers to bring their animals to the house themselves. He selected the best ones and they were butchered in Ma'Caro's compound.

That evening, the Igwe himself came to my house. For several minutes, he watched Ugbaja and his boys working like slaves on my new house, frowning as his 'limousine' continued to backfire and jerk, minutes after his driver had switched off its engine. Finally, he turned and entered Meme Jumai's house for the first time ever. He waited till the houseboy who brought the kola nut had left the room before he placed his fan on the table and leaned towards me. Is it true, what Igwe is hearing? He asked, acting like a woman whose ears had been tickled by gossip.

I told him that it depended on what Igwe had heard.

Is it true that you want to do a burial ceremony for Meme Jumai?

This very tomorrow, I told him.

He sat back and chewed his kola nut silently. After many minutes, he spoke again. It is a bad idea. Tell whoever advised you to do this thing that Igwe said it is a very bad idea.

I asked him why it was a bad idea.

He threw his kola nut away and shouted angrily, You're not a child, you're playing with abomination! The whole Ikerre-Oti joined hands to lynch your crazy father; you think they'll come to his burial feast?

I said nothing. I could hear jealousy frying his voice. He had hired fifty-two canopies for his coronation and it was the biggest party Ikerre-Oti had ever seen. Already the whole Ikerre-Oti was talking about the eighty canopies I had hired so far, which had blocked four streets — and I hadn't even finished. By tomorrow, nobody would ever mention the Igwe's coronation if the subject was big parties. That was all that was vexing him.

Leave Meme Jumai, he told me finally. He has finished what he agreed with his Maker that he wanted to do in this world. Let him go with his fate. Don't spoil your destiny with his bad luck.

So I asked him how many Ikerre people in the past had died without a burial ceremony.

He said that even Journeyman, who was so poor that he used groundnut husks for firewood, got a burial ceremony.

I asked him why it should be in my father's case that the tradition would change.

He vexed again, shouting that if I wanted him to open all his mouth, then he would, to my shame; that my father was an abomination and that if I wanted to waste my money, I should go ahead, but that any Ikerre person who attended the burial would be ostracized by his council.

I told him to speak for himself and he laughed and said that if I saw him at the burial I could marry his first daughter.

I told him that if he wanted we could bet a hundred thousand naira, or two, as I wasn't interested in any of his daughters.

He was silent for a long time. The Igwe's driver was a retired mechanic and we could hear him trying to coax the car back to life. The Igwe said in a different voice that we should leave aside the issue of his daughters, because there was a vacancy for a chief on his council and I shouldn't spoil my chances of becoming the youngest chief in Ikerre-Oti. I knew immediately that what was on top of his mind right then was the replacement of his royal vehicle.

I was also silent for a very long time, remembering the last time Pa tried to take a case to the Igwe's court. Chentus had encroached on his land. Instead of sharpening a machete like an angry Ikerre man, Pa had gone to the Igwe's waiting room to report. He was there four hours and the Igwe sent him three messengers. The first messenger said the Igwe was sleeping. The second messenger said the Igwe was eating. The third messenger said the Igwe was sleeping. After that my father had come home and gone two days without eating. And here was the same Igwe, offering me my choice of daughters and a chieftaincy stool — if only I would give Pa a lizard's burial.

I told him that anywhere I mentioned my hometown, the next question people always asked me was: Ikerre-*what*? I told him that if I wanted a chieftaincy title, I knew a couple of agents in Warri who were hawking the chieftaincies of *real* towns. That if I had a free weekend I could pick up three or four chieftaincy titles from popular towns between Onitsha and Lagos.

That was when he said he was running late for a very important meeting.

As I was seeing him off, I kicked a small carton out of the way. When I was coming back, I hissed and kicked it the other way. It's one of the cartons of money my boys unloaded from the cars yesterday; it fell down on the way to my wardrobe and I told them to leave it where it fell. Considering how money has insulted my family in this world, it hasn't seen anything yet.

24th June 2000

TODAY I TOLD UGBAJA TO suspend construction because of Pa's burial ceremony. My boys worked like animals. More goats and cows died in Ikerre-Oti today than since the beginning of harvest. Ma Caro hired six more women to cook the jollof and the smell of rice and fried meat filled the village from one end to the other.

I did my business in the daytime so as to have time for the burial. Despite all the faxes we've been sending all over the world, there's been no reply for how many days now. In the evening I picked up my Billy Barber file and read it very well. The idiot will be expecting one hundred and seventy million dollars in his bank account today. Was this man born this stupid, or is it something he did to himself? I thought and I thought and at last, I began to write:

My dearest brother, Billy,

I thank Almighty God who joined us together for this business that our millions have reached the front gate and is knocking gbam-gbam on the door of opportunity. I've now pushed our file from the Remittance Section to the Approval Section at the ministry. Yesterday, they wrote the cheque for one hundred and seventy million dollars in your name! If you see how I was shaking, my brother Billy! But the Devil has now put his ugly hand into our business. Yesterday, the DG seized the file and put K.I.V. on it!

You know that K.I.V. is a terrible killer in the ministry. Once a file carries the 'Keep In View' stamp it can be on standstill for another five years if we're not careful. Quick, quick, I called the D.G.'s P.A. and discussed business with him. Then and there, he told me that his D.G. always K.I.V.s any file with cheque inside it until he gets his own share of the money. Immediately, I took my father's title deeds to a loan shark and got two million naira (that is about eighteen thousand dollars), which I gave the D.G. You know what the thief said? He said I should bring fifteen thousand dollars more or forget about the whole thing.

So my brother Billy, that's the situation now. I have scraped even my hair into this business and if I scrape any more, it is blood that will come out. Please try to send the remaining money. As the cheque is already typed, if I get the fifteen thousand dollars in the morning, the one hundred and seventy million dollars will be in your account by evening.

Please don't disappoint me, and the two both of our future generations. Your obedient servant,

Dr. Amechi.

By the time I faxed the letter, the band I brought from Warri was already playing. Felitony and his International Megastars was one of the most popular bands around but his charges were so high that he had never played in Ikerre before. I spread the word that Felitony was coming and the Igwe spread the word that my guests would be ostracized. In the end, this is what happened:

For the first thirty minutes, Felitony was playing to empty chairs. Many villagers stood around in the darkness, but my canopies were empty. I could also see from Felitony's face that the insult was getting too much, because he had played from Potiskum to Port Harcourt and people had never refused to dance to his music before. But I knew what was driving the Ikerre people. It was Pa's coffin, which was lying beside the stage that we built for Felitony. After all, these were the same villagers that lynched Meme Jumai, it was too much to expect them to come and dance in the very presence of his corpse.

So I called my boys and we carried the coffin to the backyard. The reverend said the prayers and we put Pa's coffin into the ground. Then one of my boys entered the compound in the full view of the villagers wearing the Igwe's chieftaincy regalia, complete with his veiled cap. As he danced to the stage, Felitony started to sing the Igwe's praises. Then I danced to the stage with Egbuna carrying a carton behind me. I sprayed the singer until he started to smile again. I sprayed 'the Igwe' until people started grumbling that it was no wonder he didn't want them to come to the burial, he wanted all the money for himself. Then I turned to the empty canopies and threw handfuls of currency in the air.

That's how Meme Jumai's burial feast started. There was a stampede. First they rushed the money, then they rushed the food; by the time Felitony started to sing Meme Jumai's praises, their brains were so soaked that they saw nothing wrong with singing and dancing along. If the Igwe decided to ostracize my guests, he would have to live alone in his stupid village. Yet, just before midnight, he entered the compound angrily. His poisonous eyes didn't intimidate anybody.

Even you? He told Elder Koiki, who was dancing the stomach-dance surrounded by clapping villagers. Normally, only pregnant women could do the stomach-dance very well, but Elder Koiki was a beer drinker, and if his stomach was on a woman she would have been rushed to the labour room.

What about you? Asked Elder Koiki, who wasn't the timid type.

The Igwe didn't come for the party! He roared, The Igwe was told that somebody was impersonating me here!

Me too, said the drunk Elder Koiki, dancing on. In fact I'm not the one you're speaking to, it's my impostor.

So that is how I buried Meme Jumai; it was the biggest burial ceremony that Ikerre-Oti has ever seen — and I'm counting the burial of Barika's father three years ago. I don't think I'll be dreaming about sarcastic lizards again. That was also how I got my revenge on the people of Ikerre-Oti, but that's a different story:

25th June 2000

THE SOUND OF SHOUTING WOKE me up and when I looked into the compound, the place was full of angry people still in their loin-clothes. It was like a riot. Elder Koiki was struggling with my bodyguards, trying to reach my door. When I came out, they let him come near me.

What's the matter? I asked him.

What is the matter? He shouted, pushing me against the wall. My bodyguards held him back. There was fear inside his eyes and white spittle at the corners of his mouth. His breasts, which were like a woman's, were shaking as he struggled with my boys. You're asking me what's the matter? Everybody in my house has diarrhoea, that's the matter! Including my dog! You hear me so? And my dog ate the leftovers from your father's burial feast yesterday.

Sorry, O. I told him.

It's not a matter of sorry! He screamed. Despite that, it was difficult to hear him because everybody was screaming as well. I was just hoping that nobody would head for my cars with a gallon of petrol. It's a very serious matter, he was saying. You're going to tell me what you put in that jollof rice yesterday.

One of the angry villagers ran to my latrine. He tried the door, and when he saw there was somebody inside already, he jumped the hedge into Ma Caro's compound. I turned to Elder Koiki. We're not children, I told him; everybody knows that if you eat too much you will purge. I saw the way you were eating yesterday...

We're not children either, yelled the elder angrily, and he would have hit me again, if one of my bodyguards had not hooked his hand. The whole village can't be purging like this; yours isn't the first feast we have eaten!

But the way you were eating... I said.

But he was shouting like a madman: Confess, Calamatus! I didn't see you eating anything yesterday. What did you put inside that jollof rice? Why did you poison us?

So I told them to wait for me. I went to the hedge and hailed Ma Caro, who got the contract to cook the burial feast. These people, I told her when she came, are asking me what I put into the jollof you served them yesterday.

Why? She asked angrily, Are they saying it wasn't sweet? The rice that they rushed like refugees from warfront?

No, I told her, but they're stooling like agric fowls. They're asking what we put inside the jollof rice to make them purge like that.

She opened her mouth at Elder Koiki. She shouted: The jollof rice that I, *Mama Caro,* served from my own very pot? She loosened her head-tie and tied it around her waist, ready to fight.

That same food. I told her.

Then she hissed and bent over. She put a finger in the dust, licked it, and pointed at the sky. She opened all her eyes and began to swear and curse: I swear I didn't poison the jollof! If I did, let Caro my daughter die in childbirth! Let the child she delivers survive only to be slaughtered in a motor accident on his wedding day! As for me myself, if I poisoned the rice, let a pot of boiling oil pour over me! Let me die in prison. Let epilepsy choke me to death. If I poisoned the jollof, let my business scatter. As for anyone that says I poisoned the jollof...

Elder Koiki stopped her immediately, It's enough. Ah! I say it's enough!

They were satisfied. Even I had never heard a more terrible oath. But it can't be the beer, one of them was grumbling as Elder Koiki hurried desperately towards my latrine. I opened the beer myself. It was corked from Nigerian Breweries.

It isn't the beer, said Ma Caro, panting heavily as she tied her scarf back on her hair again. Ask me and I'll tell you: it's your greed that's killing you. Because of the sweetness of my jollof, all of you came out like goats. Shame on you. You're the same people that lynched Meme, only to come here to sing his praise and eat his funeral rice. Abomination! If killing Meme was a mistake, won't you first apologize to his relatives? Don't you know tradition? If I were Meme's spirit, I wouldn't give you ordinary diarrhoea! I'd give you haemorrhoids! If I were Meme's spirit...

The rioters disappeared quickly.

When the last one had gone I took Ma Caro to a corner: Shameless people, she was muttering, it was just a plate of food Meme was begging and they refused, but they can eat and dance in his compound.

How can you curse yourself and Caro like that? I asked, knowing her to be very superstitious.

Nothing will happen to us, she told me, as she returned to her house, I didn't put it in the jollof, I put it in the goat meat.

The labourers resumed work on the new house this morning. They had knocked down Ma's old kitchen to make way for the new house. This afternoon, I noticed some boys standing together and laughing when they were supposed to be breaking up the roof; and what I don't like is for people to be laughing on my time. I went there, and found them reading Ma's old love letters hidden in the thatch of the roof. So I seized the letters and sent them back to work.

In the night I heard a voice that was rough like sandpaper laughing between the quarrelling on the street and the quarrelling in the television. I was glad that Pa liked the joke I played on the villagers. What I don't like is that a man has to be dead before he can see anything funny about this life.

26th June 2000.

WHEN I CAME OUT OF the bathroom, my fax machine was singing again, but this time it wasn't a happy song. I took the paper and read it while I was eating. Billy Barber, the Vegas idiot was getting angry. See what he said:

Dr. Amechi,

I was extremely disappointed to receive your last fax detailing yet another hurdle between us and the profits of this business transaction. I'm afraid I can't raise the money you requested. I'm also certain that I've reached the end of my credit accommodation with my bank. Am I to understand that unless I can come up with the deposit, the deal is off? If this is so, then I demand a refund of my investment so far. When we started this transaction, (refer to your first letter of April, 2000) you made it abundantly clear that the only commitment required of me was to make my bank account available, now...

And that's how he went on, grumbling like a woman.

So I took my pen. It is now that I regret playing with my secondary school. I would have liked my letter to be smooth like that of this Barber man. If only Abel, with his first class degree, will agree to do this business with me! It's not for nothing that they call him Booker T. Instead the jobless man is fooling around, calling himself a writer. Well, I am a writer myself. He can be writing his animal stories and other nonsense, me, I will specialize in writing con letters and writing fat cheques. Besides, it's even good that my English is using walking stick: when the *mugus* read my letters they think they have seen an illiterate that they can cheat; and they'll keep thinking like that till I have finished shaving their heads for them. Idiots.

This is what I wrote:

My dear, dear brother Billy.

I was very sad to read your last fax. It was when you talked about accommodation and credit that I saw that you haven't understood what we're talking about here. My dear brother Billy, this matter has passed the problem of accommodation. I myself have sold my own house. In fact I have now secretly sold my father's house in the village for sake of this business. I don't even know what to tell my brothers when they come home for Christmas and see that our family house has become a poultry. Are you still driving a car? Sell it at once! Didn't you read my first letter of April 14th instantly? I am talking of 170 million dollars, not 170 <u>thousand</u> dollars: And how much is the final, final contribution they are asking us to make to settle the greedy D.G. who is KlVing our file? Just a chicken-change of $15,000 — when I've invested ten times that amount already.

Please just don't annoy me. With the kind of sacrifice that I am sacrificing in this country for the sake of this our joint business, it is just paining me to read your letter and to think that by tomorrow, when the money enters your account, both of us will fifty-fifty it. In fact if I were you, I'll borrow my wife's car and sell it. You can tell her that they stole it. After all, by next week you can buy her a Labroginy Cuntarsh or even a jet plane. Anyway, is it not because the cheque has been written in your name that you're now bluffing me? If you want me to go and put my neck inside the trap of another loan shark, I will, but you must agree to give me extra ten percent on top, making 60-40 instead of 50-50.

Please take your choice immediately.

Your partner in progress,

Dr. Amechi.

When I finished writing the reply, I called in Ode and he typed it out. Then I used my Dr. Amechi signature and signed it. I faxed it immediately to Billy Barber. Then I brought out my telephone directory and started showing my new apprentices how to set the traps. I used four letters, the oil letter, the contract letter, the ammunition letter, and the human rights letter. I shared out the work to all of them. Before the end of the day I had faxed one hundred letters and one hundred and fifty letters were ready for posting.

Life is good; I have to tell the truth.

While my boys were working, I filled up my pockets and took a stroll with two bodyguards. Despite yesterday's diarrhoea, everywhere I entered they were hailing me, *Ca-la-mi-ty! Ca-la-mi-ty!* And as they hailed me, that was how I sprayed them with cash.

27th June 2000

Today, I spent the morning watching my money working. The boys were writing letters and faxing them all over the world. The bricklayers and carpenters were building the fastest house in Ikerre-Oti. I sat in the shade eating boiled corn and coconut and drinking wine.

I wasn't the only person watching. For the villagers of Ikerre, the house growing in Jumai's compound is now more interesting to watch than even World Cup football. Already the house is climbing faster than any house has ever climbed in the history of Ikerre. Today, more than forty labourers are working on the site, jamming themselves like ants as they carry blocks and iron rods up and down the place. And all these girls who have no respect, their mouths are now closed like the teeth of a mousetrap. What song can they sing again? They are just sitting down there moping, like cows. And I like it like that. Let the compound of Jumai be famous for something apart from poverty and dead goats.

In the afternoon a young man brought me Pa's rifle. It was wrapped in a sack like a stick of smoked fish and he asked me whether I wanted to buy it back.

I looked at it very well. It was the very one Pa inherited from his own father. As I turned it around in my hand, I remembered that this was just the second time in my life I was holding the gun. The first time was when I climbed to the roof to play with it and Pa caught me red-handed. He had flogged me until my buttocks lost their skin.

I looked at the man. To get the gun, he must have been in the forefront of Pa's killers. Yet, he wasn't afraid to sell it to me! You can see how money mesmerizes people. Everybody wants a piece of Calamity's wealth.

I asked him if this was the same rifle that police were looking for in the 'Half-Dozen Murders Case' and he told me he was just a Second-hand Dealer who bought the gun from a customer.

I told him that some of my best friends were robbers; and that from personal experience, the difference between a robber's jail-sentence and the jail-sentence of a receiver of stolen goods wasn't long enough to grow a moustache in. I told him he could leave the gun with me and I would forget the case, or he could take it away and I would send the police after him.

He left it with me.

Idiot.

Visitors are my main problem these days. From morning until night, that's how they troop in. As soon as one pot of maize leaves the fire, they have to put another one on again.

In the afternoon, one hungry lawyer came to see me. In the middle of eating my maize, he said that the Etong family was his client and that I was in serious trouble.

I told him that if he was looking for a bribe, he had come to the wrong house.

He said there was a difference between a bribe and an out-of-court settlement.

I told him that the only thing he would get out of me was the maize that was already in his mouth.

He replied that the way I was talking wasn't the way a quarrel could be resolved.

My glass of wine was very full, so I laughed very gently but even then my cup was running over. There was a time when I might have been shaking at the threat of a lawyer. But that was a few days and many millions of naira ago. I told him that the only quarrel I knew of was the one between a dead Etong and a dead Jumai, and that since both the plaintiff and the defendant were dead, it was obviously a case for God to judge.

He didn't like how my other guests were laughing at him, so he asked me whether I took him for a fool.

I told him that it was wrong to insult a visitor to his face.

He told me that since my father had killed the breadwinner of the Etong clan at home and abroad, I should bear in mind that I had inherited his responsibility.

I told him that everything in life had an expiry date and that the quarrel between Pa and Etong had expired.

His face became ugly like an *egwugwu* mask and he asked whether he would have suffered to read law if cases were so simple to solve. He jumped up and said he was going to court, but he stood there, maybe to give me time to start begging him. I asked him if he was wanting a lift to the Courthouse along Quarry Road and he left angrily.

Later a fax came in from the Billy Barber man. This is what it said:

> *Dear Dr. Amechi,*
>
> *I got your last fax. I've have had a good think on it and I prefer the 50-50 set-up. I've raised another ten thousand dollars, but that's absolutely it. I'll transfer the money into your account and you should have the funds within the next one week. Please, please, let everything work according to plan this time around.*
>
> *Yours,*
>
> *Billy Barber.*

I read the letter very well then I took a stroll around the village, laughing like a rich man. I laughed my laughter the way children used to make their coconut biscuits last for the whole day: every time one laughter begins to finish, I take another small bite and it starts again. There's a musical way that people are hailing me on the road that can make anybody's head to swell. *Ca-la-mi-ty! Ca-la-mi-ty!* It is a song on its own.

A short but powerful song. I just wave my fan and smile. Life is good, and anyone who disagrees should feel free to jump inside River Niger.

28th June 2000

TODAY, WHEN I WOKE UP, Abel was swallowing the breakfast my houseboys had cooked for me. His clothes were dusty and rumpled, as if he had walked all the way from Warri. I looked at his eyes once and I knew he was looking for a quarrel.

He chewed a boiled egg three times and swallowed it down with pap. Somebody told me that you buried Pa some days ago, was his 'good morning' to me. He continued: I told him he was lying. Calama, tell me he's lying.

I didn't like the way he was calling me Calama. That was how Pa used to call me and Pa never called me for anything good. The phone rang two times and the fax machine started whining like an animal that had taken an arrow in the neck. The corpse of another big game was coming to my house and it made me very patient with jealous people.

I knew that what was coming out of Abel's mouth was just poverty and frustration. If you see a man who is angry all the time, check his pocket very well. If it's not poverty, it's a wife who has electric current in her tongue. Upon his first-born and first class degree, Abel is still a beggar. The kind of brain that works well inside university isn't the same kind that works well on the streets. I just pitied him. So as not to embarrass him, I sent my boys away.

Yet, before I could open my mouth, he was talking again. He

wouldn't leave my food alone and he wouldn't stop abusing me. His voice was shaking with envy: And what are you building all over the compound? You think because you've tricked money out of some innocent souls it gives you the right of first-born? If you are a *419ner* outside this house, let me tell you that I was already standing up to piss before you were born. You can't con me out of my own rights in this family!

I looked at my brother, and I must tell the truth, I finally began to vex. After all, is it my fault that he's jobless? So I stood up and poured the remaining food into the dustbin. I left him with his fork hanging in the air.

Have you just realised that you're the first-born? I asked him. Now that I've cleaned the house and put food on the table? Shameless man! Were you waiting for me to print and post you an invitation for your father's burial? When you heard he was dead, what did you think would follow? Baptism ceremony? Look, carry yourself out of this house before I call my boys, otherwise what will happen to you will surprise you.

His voice was still shaking but this time it was shame.

Calamatus, he whispered, is it me that you are talking to like this? Me, *Abel?*

I could see that he was now begging me. Like Pa, he didn't know how to say 'sorry'. I just hissed and told him that it wasn't Abel I was talking to; it was his brother Cain. Then I walked into the other room. The fax was from a new idiot from Hong Kong. His English was so bad that I couldn't understand whether he was coming or going, and I must say the truth, at this point in time I had no patience for illiterates. I had another corn roasting in the fire and if I didn't turn it immediately it was going to burn. So I put the new fax to one side and wrote a reply to the *mugu* that called himself Billy Barber.

My dear Billy Barber,

You made a typewriter's mistake in your last fax. Instead of fifteen, you wrote ten thousand dollars. I know very well that you cannot mean ten thousand dollars because a human being cannot miss one hundred and seventy million dollars because of a chicken-feed five thousand dollars small change.

Anyway, I read that fax very well, my brother, and I'll tell you the truth. If not that they've already written the cheque in your name, I would have chosen another partner from the six people who replied after you and asked them to refund the nonsense money you have invested in this business. Why are you talking about one week to transfer a nonsense fifteen thousand dollars? Money that is chicken-feed to me? Can't you understand the urgency of this matter? Don't you understand that the one hundred and seventy million dollars will reach your account the day after I receive this fifteen thousand dollars?

Please, please, please shake your body and send this money by immediate telegramic transfer. I can't believe that you are trying to save common twenty dollars transfer charges at this junction. Originally, when they told me that white men are misers I didn't believe them. It vexes me that when I am working so hard that accidental fart is coming out of me, my partner — with who I'm doing fifty-fifty — is working and blowing whistle with his mouth.

On a sweeter note, please help me to book the biggest room at any Holiday Hotel near you for next week Monday. My full name is Dr. Oliver Nzuzu Amechi and I will arrive at evening flight. Please don't try to escape with my share of the money. I don't want to arrive in Vegas and start hearing story that you went for summer holiday to Parrot or is it Canary Island. Also, help me to check the price of the most expensive Mercedes Benz on the market. That is my promise to my wife — and you know that I am a man of honour.

Your Nigerian Partner.

Dr. Amechi

By the time I returned to the parlour Abel was eating the second plate they had brought for me. He didn't look like somebody struggling for birthright anymore. In fact, later in the night, he asked me where I wanted to sleep so he could know where to sleep and I told him that the bed I used to replace Pa's clay bed was big enough for both of us.

And when you check it very well, this is my only brother. He may not have money in his pocket, but I know his mind. His problem is poverty; and the fact that he loves Ma *too* much. Imagine inviting her for his marriage when he didn't even invite Pa. That's how this stupid rumour about his going with a delegation from the vulcaniser's clan started. We have quarrelled and fought in public before but no amount of anger has made him open his mouth to expose my secrets. After all, nobody outside our compound knows why I hate women. And nobody knows that I didn't really kill that Fulani man how many years ago. Wasn't I standing beside him on that evil day, near Ubiaja, when they told us that Patie couldn't marry him because she wasn't raised to eat dead animals?

As I am writing this thing now, all I am thinking is what I'm going to do about Patie. I was still thinking that same thing when they brought me a court summons from the hungry lawyer. The date of the court is tomorrow. I laughed and tore the summons in front of the bailiff. As he left, I sent one of my boys with a paper bag full of money for the judge.

29th June 2000

WHEN I WOKE, I TOLD Abel everything that was in my belly. His head was going up and down like a car whose shock absorber was broken. Then he asked, What about Patie? Will she still come with me after that?

I thought very well, then I brought down my feet from the carton I was using as a stool. I opened it for Abel to see. Keep this at home, I told him. If she doesn't come back to you, she will come back to the money.

My brother scratched his head. You don't know what Patie can do. He said.

But I know what money can do. I told him.

We agreed on a date and that same morning Abel returned to Warri. It was at the door, as he was going, that we nearly quarrelled again. He said he was going to invite Ma and her manfriend for the marriage!

I looked at him.

I told him that if she was coming, then I wasn't going to be there. He was still arguing about that so I brought out the letters, my labourers found in the roof of Ma's kitchen when they pulled it down to dig the foundation for my guest chalet. They were all in Ma's handwriting. I selected one addressed to 'Honey-Joe' and put it in his hand. This was what it said.

12 January 1974.

My dearest Honey-Joe,

Why are you doing me like this now? Upon all the letters that I write to you, why can't you reply even one line? If you hear that Stella has died, you shouldn't just sorry at all because is you that has killed me. You know that my mind is with you all the time. Honey-Joe, so you're still angry because I began to friend the farmer? I only did that because I was jealousing how you were friending that seamstress on Willoughby Street. I know people are telling you that you shouldn't mind Stella again, that she's married, but is only deposit that the farmer paid on my head, he hasn't paid the full bride price.

I know that the seamstress is still poisoning your mind, saying that Stella has borned, that she is old cargo, but that is nonsense. My stomach is as you remember it — and the child I had on Christmas day, he's actually your son. You should see his nose. And if you don't believe your nose, if you like, calculate it. Is just because I was angry with you that I gave him to the farmer. But if you prefer us to start again from the start, me I don't mind at all, Honey-Joe, is you I want. I can leave the farmer with his bastard even this tomorrow, just give me eye, that's all. My love is strong like River Niger and am waiting to carry you away inside it.

Your darling.

Honey-Stella.

This my brother's mind is water, true. He left the house without talking, but I've seen his eyes. I know that he will be crying from here to Warri. I don't think Stella Jumai — or is it Stella-Joe — will be attending his traditional marriage anymore.

Later that morning they brought one of the new boys to me. His head was shaped like a mango and his eyes had very deep sockets, as if they were planted by catapult. They said he was the most intelligent student at grammar school and that only his parents' poverty kept him from university. I wasn't surprised. After all, he has nothing to distract him from his studies.

What's the matter? I asked them, and they told me how, instead of copying the simple letters I gave them to copy he was busy correcting them. So I asked him what specie of demon was pushing him to destroy my business.

He said he was trying to make the con sound better; that no reasonable person would swallow it as it was.

I looked at the boy. If they told you that a monkey was his father you won't doubt it. I told him to step outside and look around the compound. He did so. My new house had passed the lintel level and was growing furiously. The salesman at the Warri car lot had discovered my address and he has sugar in his tongue. Already there were four long cars in front of my house — not counting the one I returned to FazO and the one I gave to Abel.

If I can do this with foolish letters, I asked Mangohead when he returned into the house, why do you want to spoil it with your intelligence? Can you eat intelligence? Can you wear it like a dress?

He listened, which made me know that he will go far. After all, intelligence is useful in the business as well, but one has to know how to apply it. Didn't the mother of two sons sell the fool to ransom the thief? I decided to give the boys a small lecture. I looked at the letter again: A corrupt minister had just died, leaving millions of dollars in a secret Zurich bank account. His second wife who was a signatory was looking for assistance to get the money out without the knowledge of the government and the first wife.

What's your problem with this letter? I asked him.

Why can't the woman find a friend to go and get the diamonds? Why should she trust someone she's never met before with 80 million dollars worth of diamonds?

Because she's supposed to be foolish. I told him. *Mugus* always think they're wise, the more foolish you appear, the more comfortable they'll be with you.

But it's so... foolish! No reasonable man will believe it! Protested Mangohead.

If the price is right, I told him, most people in the world will agree to do one foolish thing, especially if it is in secret.

This boy was stubborn. He said: But Sir, I've written three hundred letters so far and nothing-nothing.

I laughed. Even yams need months before you can harvest them, I told him. Look, if out of ten thousand letters one idiot agrees to send me ten thousand dollars, what does that make me?

A millionaire. Said Mangohead.

I asked him how many yams he would have to plant to harvest ten thousand dollars worth and with all his intelligence he couldn't even calculate that. So I told him that if he was looking for a place to plant his intelligence, he should try his father's farm. Then I sent them away.

Later, I sent for Chief Ato and we discussed Abel's traditional marriage for a long time. He said 'No' many times, but every time he said 'No', I put another bundle of naira on the table. Eventually, he brought out a nylon bag from his pocket. As he packed away his money, he was grumbling that he didn't even know where to find the head of a bat.

I didn't bother to answer that one.

After that, I sent Egbuna to find out the judgment of the customary court in the case filed for the Etongs by the hungry lawyer. He returned to say that the case had been adjourned till tomorrow. The judge had a headache.

30th June 2000

ANOTHER FAX CAME FROM BILLY Barber today. I would have pitied the young man, but the truth about this life is that a human being has to sympathize with himself first, before knowing whether he has enough sympathy for other people. I don't have enough sympathy for me and Billy Barber. Anyway, I don't like greedy people. For a man to think he can get eighty-five million dollars just because he has a bank account! He should be punished for his greed! He should be flogged and sent to a psychiatric hospital! This is what the fool had to say today.

I'm stewing right now, Dr. Amechi. Let me tell you how I got the last dough I sent you. It was my office provident fund. I even borrowed Harry Baumer's signature to pull it out of the bank. Now, there's an emergency committee meeting and I got to get it back right away. Dr. Amechi, am I getting through? I'm not flogging the $170,000,000.00 deal right now. I am talking about the very last $10,000 and $5,000 I sent you. I must have it back like yesterday. Let me spell it out real simple, Dr. Amechi, if I don't have that money wired in by tomorrow evening I'll be arrested. You know what that means for our business: I can't cash your share of the money from the pen — and you know the check is already in my name. Please, Dr. Amechi, I know you are a considerate man of honour, wire the bucks back *into my account. Even if you can't meet the bank charges, send the fourteen thousand, nine hundred and eighty dollars. I'll be checking my account every hour.*

Yours truly, Billy Barber.

When I finished reading this letter I was sad to the centre of my belly, because I knew very well that my Billy Barber account was about to close. Then I filed and forgot about it.

I sent off two boys to hire buses for Abel's marriage party. I sent others to buy the cows, the yams and the goats. I gave Ma Caro another cooking contract.

These villagers are totally useless people. Look at Jared the Tailor for instance. He refused to sew any clothes for the Jumai family for the last six years just because Pa took five months to pay for our 1994 Christmas outfits. Today, laughing that his laughter that sounds like a tired sewing machine, he brought three expensive robes for me to 'test'. When we were almost naked he wouldn't give us credit. Now that I have cartons of things that I haven't even worn once, see what this creep is doing, this miser that uses the remnants from his customers' materials to sew himself handkerchiefs. See how useless this world is?

Egbuna returned from the court with the message that the judge had adjourned the case again because of his toothache. Yet, for the next fifteen minutes he was polishing the new fridge, so I knew that something else was biting his mind. What's the matter? I asked him.

It's this traditional marriage of a thing. He said finally. It's good as we're going to marry a wife for Abel, after all, he's your senior brother. But it will be good for us to marry a wife for you as well, Sir. After all, the cars are there. The house is there. The money is there. He paused, then he added sullenly, After all, this is Ikerre, Sir. A bachelor has no dignity. There should be a madam in this house, Sir.

I just started shouting at the boy, abusing him, telling him to mind his own business; asking if he hadn't seen men that marriage had destroyed. I was yelling, saying that what my mother did to my father, no woman would ever do to me. In fact I was shouting for a long time after he had run away. Finally I kept quiet. Because what was inside me wasn't vex at all, only bitterness that was very deep like a well.

The day I discover that midwife, I'll kill her. By God!

Near midnight, my fax machine woke me up. By the time I reached it, another letter was coming out:

Dr. Amechi,

I can see now that you're a thoroughgoing bastard. You are an illiterate, conniving, pimping bastard. Your relatives are reptiles. You are a snake yourself and I'll see you in hell. Unless that money hits my account in the next twenty-four hours, I'll be on the next plane to your country. Africa's ass isn't deep enough for you to hide from me, you faggot. I'll get INTERPOL on your ass so *fast you won't know what hit you. I'll take out a Mafia contract on you. They'll chop you into steaks and spare ribs for* zoo *dingoes. You think I'm a sucker? Well, you just wait. You have six hours to wire that money into my account, you read me? SIX HOURS! I'm not going to jail for any defrauding, reptilian bastard like you. I'll see you in jail first, may you rot in hell.*

Your worst nightmare, Billy (The Blade) Barber.

I threw it away. Billy The Blade Barber indeed. He should have called himself Billy the scissors barber. Nonsense. It is now that razor blades and daggers will be appearing from his name. Am I supposed to wet my trouser because of that? Some people have no shame. What has happened has happened. Why *mugus* always dig up graves looking for what isn't there anymore is what I can never understand. I waited for another hour to see whether the trap I had set in Hong Kong would bring anything, but nothing-nothing. I went to bed.

1st July 2000

I waited from 8 am to 11 pm but the fax machines didn't talk again. The Hong Kong man had climbed into his shell like a snail that licked salt by mistake. All the other traps we've been setting since how many days now, nothing-nothing. I began to sweat. Billy Barber's money was like a well but one day it will dry. I have seen conmen whose luck flashed only once. Poverty is very wicked to people who return to her after tasting real money. It isn't good for a career to end at the very junction that it started. At the last, I went back to the dustbin and found Billy's last fax. I turned it up and I turned it down. I read that letter and I read it again. Then I put it down and brought out my pen. Then I began to write.

FazO taught me that a conman should never stop taking from a *mugu* until the *mugu* stops giving to the conman. Billy Barber hasn't stopped giving. True, he says he has no more money, but those white people never have money anyway, what they have is credit, and that's enough for me.

I wrote the letter three times, but I wasn't happy, so I called Mangohead and he polished the letter till I was happy. Then Ode typed it on 'Tijani's' letterhead and faxed it through the second telephone line:

Dear Mr. Barber.

Greetings from the C.I.D. headquarters in Nigeria. I am

so delighted to tell you that the conman who was calling himself Dr. Amechi has now been trapped in my Police net. My team has been tailing him for many weeks and we closed him yesterday. I was searching his office when your last fax came and I put two and two together to get five (he laughs).

I am so happy to tell you that I was alone in the office when your fax arrived; consequently I have the option to take this matter like a private matter. Mr. Barber, I pitied you when I realized that you were one of the victims of this international fraudster, alias Dr. Amechi (where did a semi-illiterate like him finish primary school, not to talk of doctorate degree!). But I am sad to tell you that if you come to this country as you were thinking, we will have to arrest you as soon as your plane arrives, because the plan you were making with the fake Dr. Amechi is a very serious offence here. However, I am happy to say that there's a Sharia option to the Life Imprisonment sentence: that is amputation. You can opt to forfeit either one leg or one arm instead of wasting away in jail.

However, I am so delighted to tell you that as I was searching the house of the fake Dr. Amechi, I found his savings account passbook. He had three hundred and sixty thousand US dollars inside it. Could this be yours? Officially, I am supposed to hand this into the office, because we arrested him for another fraud case involving more than six hundred thousand yen belonging to one Japanese businessman who died of heart attack last week.

Anyway, I pitied you after reading your fax. What I want to do for you, if you will agree, is to torture the fake Dr. Amechi in the cell this night until he signs a withdrawal form for the money. I plan to use needle method because we always explain the tiny marks that we leave by saying that the prisoner was a drug addict. I'm in the Special Police Squad in charge of International Scams and it has worked many times. I hope you're not a member of Amnesty International, because I don't want this plan to leak and embarrass my country and I. If you agree with this plan, you must be quick, because the case will be out of my hands by tomorrow evening. You have to send me a notarised declaration saying how much of the three hundred and sixty thousand dollars is yours. — You see, I have to protect myself. Then you have to agree to pay me twenty-percent finder's fees. You can fax your answer and the declaration as soon as possible.

Please don't write to the C.I.D. headquarters about this matter. Don't jeopardize my career just because I took pity on you.

Yours truly,

Inspector Tijani.

P.S. But how can you be so stupid to believe that hundred and seventy million dollars story? Don't you read the papers?

In the afternoon, I chartered three buses, a pick-up and a truck for the cows and goats and we went to the village near Ubiaja for Abel's traditional marriage. We went with all my cars, plus the one I gave Abel. I didn't have to beg any villager to follow us; as Mama Caro loaded her food on the pick-up, that's how the people continued to pack themselves into the buses until there was no space anymore. I can see now that the brains of Ikerre people are located inside their stomachs. Despite the diarrhoea last time, the smell of jollof rice has brought them out again.

Felitony's band had been playing there since morning. By the time we arrived at 3 pm the place was full. It was like a festival. The canopies that were there! The high table that they set! And if you saw their dancers! And if you saw their chiefs! They welcomed us and we exchanged food and drinks, but because of our plan, Chief Ato took one bite of their food and left it alone.

The story of Calamity's money had reached the village before us, and with the robe that Jared made for me, nobody needed to ask: which one is Calamity? The musicians put my name in the songs. These musicians can make somebody's head to swell! I stood up and sprayed them with money. Everybody was chanting *Ca-la-mi- ty! Ca-la-mi-ty!* The women of the village began their own beauty parade. I don't need a first class degree like Abel to know what they are planning in their mind. Even my boys were already saying that it will be good for us to come back for another marriage in this village. I swallowed my Adam's apple and said nothing.

Then the time for speeches came.

They had put me and my brother on the high table, but look at Abel's face! It was as if he was attending his own burial instead of his traditional marriage. On our way he had begged me to forget the quarrel I was planning to pick with his in-laws and let the marriage go smoothly, because he now loved Patie and didn't want anything to disturb their marriage. I had to agree with him. But I know what is inside my mind. This Abel of a man is too soft, true. He's not like a first-born at all. Before all this Patie nonsense began, he was famous in Ikerre as the only first class graduate in the village. Now he is notorious as the dead-goat-husband. For these people to disgrace our family and for him to want to forget it just like that, for the sake of a woman! Of which there're so many of them! I told him: Okay, let's forget everything. But I knew what was inside my mind, and I didn't stop Chief Ato.

It was time for speeches. My boys paraded the cows and the drinks and the yams as the speeches began. Patie's people said wonderful things about us, like people who had found famous in-laws. Money is a wonderful thing. If you heard them singing our praises, you wouldn't believe that this was the same place we came two months ago and they insulted and drove us out.

I looked at Patie's father. The man had painted his house from head to toe, and he was smiling as if Billy Barber's money was already sitting inside his account. I began to pity him, true. This is how terrorists must feel — that is, those of them who still have blood in their veins — when they enter a plane and everybody is smiling, and reading novels, and cleaning their mouths with napkins, and cutting their fish with fork and knife, not knowing that when the plane reaches quarter to Heaven it will explode.

Chief Ato stood up and took their microphone. He hacked and

spat on the ground. His eyes were shining because of all the whiskey that he had used to charge himself — and I didn't blame him at all. The kind of lies that he was going to tell, nobody can say them in his right mind.

Chief Ato began to talk. Every two or three words, he would hack and spit on the ground. Because of all the kola nut he had been chewing, his spittle was black like faeces. This is what he said: My fellow chiefs, for more than forty years I've been travelling all over Nigeria making marriages for Ikerre-Oti children, but I've never seen the kind of insult that I received today.

The noise of the party ended as if there was a power failure. The music just died, *kpam.* Mouths were dropping open all over the place. People were looking at Chief Ato as if he had gone mad. Then he lifted the plate of soup that they served him and poured it slowly on the white tablecloth. He used his fork to pick one of the pieces of meat on the cloth; when he lifted the head of a bat, people started screaming! I could see that Abel wasn't happy at all, but what he doesn't know is that all this is for his own good. When he and his wife quarrel and she calls him 'eater of dead goat meat' he can also call her 'eater of dead bat meat'; after all, which one is worse, to eat a dead goat or to eat a dead bat?

Chief Ato was shouting now, waving the head of the bat, screaming: *Abomination! Abomination!!* He was calling people to see the kind of meat our so-called in-laws had served us, asking if there was any place in this world where human beings eat bat flesh. The Ikerre villagers, who didn't know what I planned with Chief Ato, were already vomiting and rolling on the ground. This Chief Ato is a wonderful actor, true. Even me that planned it with him, the way he was talking, I began to wonder whether truly he had found a bat's head in his soup. Before you can say 'bat-soup', the kind of fight that started in that place? Hm. It was even worse than what I planned.

So that was how the whole ceremony scattered. We carried our cows and left. The only problem was that Patie refused to follow us. I told Abel to give her twenty-four hours, that she'll be back, but as he left Ikerre for his one-room house in Warri, he was looking as if it was a bad thing I did for him.

You can see the uselessness of human beings. I have organized for him the biggest traditional marriage that any Ikerre person, living or dead has ever had. I have brought back his dignity. Now, if somebody wants to describe him, Abel is no more 'that one whose in-laws disgraced over a dead goat'. He's now 'that one who disgraced his in-laws over a dead bat'. Normally, an Ikerre man who wanted to pay dowry went with a goat or two; what dowry did I give Abel? Two cows and eight goats! Yet, did the jobless man say thank you? No. He just left as if he was quarrelling with me.

This night, the boy I sent to the court to check on the Etongs' case reported that the case was adjourned till tomorrow. The judge had diarrhoea.

CALAMA

2nd July 2000

THIS MORNING, I WAS WATCHING them pour the concrete for the decking of my new house when Egbuna returned with Ode from the market. He was very angry and was breathing like someone who had just escaped from baboons. I could see he had been fighting. His face was swollen and his shirt was torn. What's the matter? I asked him.

It was Ode who replied, and Ode was very angry as well: We met Old Teacher on the way and Egbuna slapped him two times without no any reason at all — but some people saw him and they beat him up.

I looked at Egbuna, for him to tell me that it was a lie, but he was just standing there. He was panting like a man who had just finished the race of life and was waiting for his heart to catch up with him. Of all my boys, it was only Egbuna whose anger was not like matches; so what I was hearing really surprised me. So I said, Tell me what happened. Did you really slap Old Teacher for no reason at all?

I slapped him Sir, but I have a very big reason after all.

There was no any reason! Shouted Ode angrily. I saw everything!

That was when my second telephone rang and its fax machine started to sing. I adjourned my court immediately, because I don't play with my work at all. The fax was from Billy Barber and see what he said:

My dear Inspector Tijani,

I am so relieved that there is one true man left in that shambolic country, who will agree to do something without an advance fee. You can't believe my delight at the news that that dastardly conman has finally got his just desserts. I hope they chuck him in jail and melt down the keys! Better still, I hope he is tried under one of those excellent decrees and decapitated.

To turn to more urgent matters, my dear Inspector, I am prepared to handle this matter entirely as you have suggested. I assure you I'll keep this matter strictly under wraps. I wouldn't dream of breathing a word of this deal to your superiors at the CID Headquarters — and to hell with Amnesty International. If it is necessary to castrate that conman, so be it. However, regarding the finders fee you mentioned, I'm more than prepared to offer you ten percent of the three hundred and sixty thousand dollars, which is the internationally accepted percentage for recovery matters.

I am sending the notarisation for the money as you have instructed. The conman took a total of four hundred thousand dollars from me, so any other money you find is mine. You can't imagine my relief at your intervention; I was almost going round the bend. Hopefully, I won't end up like that criminal's Japanese victim! I've had my first night's sleep in weeks and look forward to receiving my funds in account soon. Do you think this will be possible by tomorrow? Yours truly,

Billy Barber.

P.S. Please could you kindly investigate the $170 million transaction very well? I did see some certified true copies that looked quite authentic. At the least can you confirm that there's no check in my name for $170 million at the Ministry of Petroleum Resources? We can also handle this on the internationally accepted percentage for recovery matters. Thank you for your understanding.

I was angry when I finished reading the fax. There's no honesty left in this world! How can the same human being be so foolish and so greedy at the same time? Claiming that he gave me four hundred thousand when I didn't even see half of that amount! If I had a partner in this business, that's how he would have caused suspicion between us. How will God even pity this kind of crook?

I saw very well that the fish was hooked. While my head was cooking the reply, I went out and listened to Egbuna's story: His father had tried to enrol him fifteen years ago at the comprehensive school where Old Teacher was the principal. Everything was going fine until Old Teacher rejected the boy's name. Egbuna's full name was Onyemegbunam but the new computer form from the Ministry had only ten spaces. Egbuna's father refused to cut two letters off the boy's name and Old Teacher refused to register the full name. It started 'like-a-joke, like-a-joke' but in the end, Egbuna didn't go to secondary school.

You're lying. I told him.

I swear, he said, that's why I couldn't be a doctor after all. Every time I meet that Old Teacher, I'm going to give him two slaps for those two spaces on his stupid form.

The other boys began to mock Egbuna, saying that enrolling in school wasn't the problem but graduating from it; that all the secondary schools in the world won't turn a dunce into a doctor, that if he was looking for someone to slap, his father was there, who refused to cut his name to Egbuna, which was what he was now called anyway.

As for me, I couldn't say anything to Egbuna. After all, when I meet the midwife that castrated me, two slaps are what I will give myself personally, to wake myself up properly for the things to follow. That is the day that I will justify the nickname I've been using since I posed with the corpse of the cattle herder.

But by then, the letter that was cooking in my head was done and I sent them away. Within two hours Mangohead had finished polishing the letter. I read it many times before I phoned my bank agent for another account number. I copied it to the bottom of the fax, then I faxed it though the second telephone number. This is what I said.

My dear Billy Barber,

I was very happy to get your fax and to see that you're serious about this business of ours. Unfortunately, when I went to the cell this morning to interrogate the fake Dr. Amechi, I found that he had attempted to escape and has now been transferred to the Maximum Security Prison where every interrogation is under CCTV (he frowns). My dear Billy Barber, in fact, I pity you for the kind of bad luck that has been following you around all this time. You see, the matter is now completely out of my hands. Because of the great pity that I have for you, I told the Prison Commandant (who is my cousin's in-law) about you. You can't believe that the greedy man wants fifteen thousand dollars up-front just to arrange for me to interrogate the fake Dr. Amechi in his private office. In fact he told me that you should transfer the money into his bank account, whose details I copied to the bottom of this fax.

Personally speaking, I don't like bribing public servants. For me, I think that you should just forget about the whole thing. After all, the way they've been raping and beating that fake Dr. Amechi in prison, he won't survive another one week. With all the debts on your head now, by the time you find the money to pay my cousin's greedy in-law, one week might have passed, Dr. Amechi will be dead and the money will pass to his illiterate wife.

I wish you good luck in your next business. Don't be very sad, at least Dr. Amechi will soon be dead and it is his illiterate wife, not him, who will enjoy your hard-earned money. And what can she do with it, if not to be carrying young college boys until one of them gives her AIDS and that will be the end of all of them. But if you're still interested in this money, maybe you should come yourself and get it, after all, if you have a very good lawyer, even if they cut off your right hand you still have the documents to prove that it's your money, not so? Please destroy all the faxes I've sent you, I don't want any trouble, you know I was just trying to help you and it is not my fault that it didn't work. As for the international percentage that you talked about, as you can see, we should have waited to catch the monkey before sharing his meat. I hope you like monkey meat. (He laughs)

Yours truly,

Inspector Tijani.

I went outside. The decking was complete. For the next few days, while waiting for the concrete to set, the workers would be finishing up the ground floor. I wish I could have packed in yesterday! I'm tired of this old house!

One of my boys returned from the customary court. The customary court judge had sat at last. His judgment was one sentence long: He had gone to school with both Meme Jumai and Ebong Etong and was too closely connected to both of them. He therefore transferred the case to a magistrate court in Sapele. My boy who went to court told me that the Etongs were grumbling outside the court that he should have known that before he ate their bribe.

Life is good; I have to tell the truth.

3rd July 2000

There's a lot of noise in the village this morning because of the assassination of the member of the House of Reps for Ikerre North. Everybody is talking about it, because there'll be a big by-election soon. Personally I've no time for politics. It's too dangerous a way to make money. I opened a bottle of champagne in the early morning and carried a chair to Pa's grave. I poured him plenty of libation. At least, if he didn't drink champagne when he was alive, let him drink it in the grave. Then I sat down and commiserated with him until the sun became too hot.

It's funny how Pa and I became friends only after he died. Part of it is that everyone has changed since my money arrived. I can't really talk *with* human beings again. When people speak to me I can see that it's really the money in my pocket they're addressing. But Pa's sandpaper voice has not changed.

Barika was my surprise visitor today. When he entered the compound, I saw how he was walking sideways like a crab, and I remembered that after all he wasn't the only trader nicknamed *No Credit Today, Come Tomorrow.* He was just an ordinary, selfish businessman doing his business when Pa went crazy and shot him in the Village Square. I started to pity him. I told him to sit down and he refused, saying that since my father shot him in the buttocks, he doesn't sit anymore, and he wasn't going to lie down in Meme Jumai's house.

I told him that this was now Calamatus Jumai's house.

We shall see about that. He said.

I didn't understand what he meant, so I told him that if he had loaned Pa the two kilograms of semolina he was begging for, all this nonsense wouldn't have happened.

He said I should stop that nonsense; that apart from the *fifty*-kilogram bag of semolina that Meme Jumai took on credit on the 12th of June, he had also loaned my father fifty thousand naira on the security of the very house and compound we were sitting inside; and this was during the planting season, in front of many witnesses.

As I looked at Barika, the reason why I hated him began to come back to me. It was that very day that I got my nickname, Calamity. I had seen a dead cattle herder and his ten cows and all that entered my mind was how to win a nickname. Barika was one of the last villagers to arrive but as soon as he saw the cows, he immediately 'recognized' the dead man as 'Ali', a cattle herder whom he gave money to go and buy ten cows for him from Zaria.

It was a bloody lie of course, but that was how Barika took over the wealth that should by rights have entered the Jumai family — whether by the law of defeat in battle or by the law of finding and keeping. That was how this thief left the roadside with ten cows and this fool left with torn clothes and a stupid nickname.

Now, if that's not a calamity, then I don't know what 'calamity' means. That old vex came back to me as I asked him how a bullet in his buttocks managed to damage his brains.

He said there was no madness in this matter at all, because even the madness my father faked at the Square was just a plot to kill him so that the borrowed money would be his own for ever — except that Pa's god was dead, whereas his own was very alive. He said that to cut a long story short, he had come to collect his money — and the interest it had gathered — which was now eighty thousand naira.

(What annoys me is that if someone *tries* to steal fifty naira at night, he will be lynched, but people like Barika will practise their daylight robbery and call it business.) I told him that all my life I had known him to be a shopkeeper and even though he had conned ten cows from me before, I was only a boy then.

He said he was also a moneylender and he had my father's signature on his register; that I must have discovered his money in my father's compound, because the whole of Ikerre knew me to be a pauper's son, so where was all the money coming from?

I told him that if he really wanted to know the source of my money, I would accept his son as an apprentice, but that from what I was seeing, he himself had no future in the business.

That was when he started to curse me. I think that old man had seen death running towards him and he was looking for a millionaire's house to die inside, to get his wife a pension or something. My boys heard the noise and came inside. They heard the abuse coming from Barika's mouth and they fell on him before I could say anything.

They beat saliva out of his mouth. I ordered them to stop but it is like those boys are headstrong; they beat him until the black of his eyes began to roll and people rushed in from the road to rescue him. Even then, they were still angry and when I ordered them to carry Barika to the dispensary and treat him, they just took him outside and dumped him there.

That's what happened, between me and my gravestone, but when the story came back to me in the morning, I couldn't believe it.

4th July 2000.

FIRST THING IN THE MORNING, a message came from the Igwe that if my hand was already carrying food to my mouth, it should return to the plate until I finished attending the court in his palace.

Since it was the same Igwe that refused to pay me the bet he lost over Pa's burial, I told my boys to cook breakfast for me *and* the Igwe's messenger. It was while we were eating that another fax came from Billy Barber.

My Dear Inspector Tijani.

I've just lost my job. Only last night, I was summoned by the board and given one week to return all the funds I took from the office funds or face prosecution. You can't imagine my present predicament. I must have that money back. Inspector, I have had to confess to my wife and she has raised a $15,000.00 loan from her bank. I lied to her that I was paying the money into the office. Inspector; I've transferred it to your Prison Commandant's account. I respect your feelings about corrupting the morals of public servants, but with due respect, inspector, they are already corrupted. In any case, please make an exception for me. <u>I must have all my money back immediately:</u> please, Inspector, my marriage depends on it. My sanity depends on it. Please don't restrict yourself to the needle *method; use the razor blade method as well. In fact, if you have to yank off that bastard's fingernails, just let him to sign the papers and transfer the balance of $324, 000, less your 10%, to my account as soon as possible. I'll be checking with my bank from this evening. Thank you very much indeed.*

Yours truly,

Billy Barber.

As I filed the fax and stood up to go to the Igwe's palace, I wasn't even smiling. There's a difference between your first million and all the others that follow. Two or three dozen boys were waiting to escort me to the Igwe's palace, but when I stepped out of my house, a convoy of expensive black cars with dark-tinted windows arrived at the compound. I went to the longest car and opened the door for FazO.

Although he didn't finish Standard Six, FazO's English and his moustache were as sharp as that of a barrister. His praise name is 'Gallon', because that's the minimum quantity of wine he will drink at a sitting. He arrived with Heartattack and some other members of our syndicate and his bodyguards shot several bullets into the air to let Ikerre-Oti know that a great man had entered their midst.

Despite all his money, FazO has a complex or something. The worst thing he hates is for anyone to call him a thief. He spends a lot of money getting close to big politicians and serious businessmen. Me, I don't mind if people call me a monkey — so long as I still have my money. I showed him my new building before taking him into my parlour for entertainment.

While I was showing him the new house I whispered to Egbuna to quickly go and spread a small Persian rug in front of my special chair. Later, I sat FazO on the chair. As he drank my wine and ate the poultry that had quickly died for him, he told me I had insulted him by buying him a new car just because something happened to the old one. That when brothers were eating from the same plate it wasn't necessary to burn a candle.

I told him I was sorry, and to prove it, I gave him the keys of another car.

He told me to remind him of my age, and I said twenty-five.

He whistled and said that I was walking the walk of a thirty-five-year old man.

I said *Gallooon!* and we all laughed. He opened another bottle of wine and poured libation again. He poured libation from every bottle he opened. Although he wasn't yet fifty, he had numerous chieftaincy titles and liked to behave like an elder.

As he poured another tot on my rug, he was saying: Conmen and thieves, — that's what white men call us! But a soldier that kills and seizes a whole country in war, is he a thief and a murderer?

No sir! We shouted.

Well, this is war. He said. The next dash of wine from his glass cost me fifty thousand naira, because it missed the dark Persian rug and hit the white carpet. FazO didn't notice: That war they started five hundred years ago, when they carried our forefathers into slavery and raped our country, we're still fighting it today, and we shall win!

Amen! We shouted, as the wine began to circulate again.

Heartattack was rubbing his large stomach. His name used to be Idris until three years ago when he hit his own money and collapsed in front of the fax machine that gave him the good news, right there in the business centre on Allen Avenue. He was unconscious when they rushed him to hospital, but even the surgeon couldn't pull the fax from his fingers. As for me, he said softly, I'm not fighting to win any war, I'm just filling my stomach.

When you're fighting a giant, asked FazO, and your head is only as high as his thighs, where do you bite him?

His thighs, answered Heartattack.

FazO filled his mouth with chicken. I'm chewing the thighs of the giant, he said. The war started before we were born and it will continue after we die; but we must win our own battles!

Amen! we shouted.

Then he turned to me and said that my star was very good, that many of the boys who had spent five years in the business had not hooked my kind of *mugu.* He gave me a list of names and addresses of the police officers, magistrates and government people on the 419 network. He said that the con artists who got into trouble were those who ate alone.

I told him that I already had the list, that money was for spending, and that any hand in that state that had the authority to sign an arrest warrant with my name on it had already eaten from Billy Barber's money.

After that he took me into my inner room and told me that politics was spoiling business for us and that Central Bank was investigating some members of the syndicate.

I asked him which members, and he said that these were big politicians whose names were too sensitive to mention in broad daylight. He said that many of the bank's ledgers had been shredded and since my name was still unknown to the investigators, huge sums had been quickly lodged in my account, which I should retransfer when the investigation was over.

I told him that he could trust me with his life.

He told me that as these syndicate members were his seniors, he was actually trusting me with something more serious than his life, but that the way I replaced his old Mercedes with a new one showed him that I wasn't the kind of person whose feet could be swept from the ground by a river of money.

When he was going, I asked my boys to load his boot with cartons of currency. He asked, what is it again? And I told him it was just the way the house of the apprentice greeted the car of the master. He laughed and said I was walking the walk of a forty-five-year old man.

I said to him, *Gallooon!* and we laughed.

Then, the villagers who had gathered around my house because of the gunshots began to chant: *Ca-la-mi-ty! Ca-la-mi-ty!* I raised my hand and they stopped obediently, to allow me to talk to my important visitor. That was when he stopped and closed his eyes until only the whites were showing. Then he asked me what I thought about politics.

I told him that after watching Chief Ato at my brother's native marriage, I had seen that standing before a whole village and telling them lies to their face was a gift that I didn't have, and that I preferred to do it in writing; and in private.

He said that from what he was seeing, if it wasn't that he already had a candidate, I would have been the next Member of the House of Representatives for Ikerre North.

I laughed and told him that I wasn't even old enough.

He said that a Sworn Declaration could have fixed that. After that I just kept quiet, because I knew that what was talking to me at that point was two or three gallons of wine.

At the Igwe's palace, Barika was waiting and I wasn't surprised. The only part of his body that wasn't under plaster of Paris was under bandage. What won't human beings do to win sympathy! The room was hissing as if it was full of serpents and all the faces that looked at me were even uglier than their mothers made them. Before I even sat down, the Igwe was shouting: Calamatus Jumai! So you and your father planned together to kill this poor man!

I told the Igwe that since he was already giving judgment it seemed I had missed my own trial.

He said no, that the case was just starting. So Barika repeated his nonsense of the day before, ending with how the villagers rescued him from assassination by my thugs. He brought his witnesses: his loan register and fifteen people who swore they saw Meme Jumai take the loan and promise to pay on the week of harvest. Now it wasn't eighty thousand naira that the snake was claiming, it was hundred and eighty thousand! Plus he brought papers that he said that Pa had signed, securing the loan with my land!

Edna and Dumbili, the two people Pa had mentioned in his diary, had already given evidence for Barika. When it was my turn to defend myself, all I could say was, Lies! Lies! Today, I was the *mugu*.

After our arguments the Igwe told us to come for judgement the next day. By the time I reached home the news had spread that Barika had offered the Igwe half of any money he got from me.

One hundred and eighty thousand naira. That was like weekend money for me. Yet, if I lost the case Barika would go around claiming that his money was what made Calamity rich — and he would have showed the people of Ikerre-Oti the newest way to make money. So I sent for Ugbaja. I told him what to say and he left my house straight for the Igwe's palace.

In the evening, I got news from Warri that Abel had had an accident in the car I gave him. His right arm was in p.o.p. and the remnants of the car could fit inside a small portmanteau. That serves him right. Ungrateful beast of a man. His whole arm should have cut off.

5th July 2000

THIS MORNING, THE IGWE'S PALACE was fuller than ever. The Igwe himself couldn't look at me, and I'm not surprised. Yesterday Ugbaja had warned him that he was playing with his new palace: that I had already paid him a deposit to build a real palace for Ikerre-Oti after my own house was finished.

Barika was there with his whole family and he was accepting congratulations as though he had already won the case. But when our chief started his judgment, I could see that this was one thief who didn't do things half-and-half.

As soon as he opened his mouth, he started to abuse Barika: that anybody who knew Meme Jumai before he died would see that the poor man hadn't seen one thousand naira together in the same place for many years. He asked what kind of greed would push Barika — who was already a rich man, although not by my standards — to lie against a dead man just to defraud a hard-working tycoon young enough to be his own son; adding that he wasn't surprised — wasn't it the same Barika who crept into his palace yesterday, as the whole village might have heard already, to try and bribe him over this very case?

Barika's anger as he left the palace twisted his face the way Pa's double barrel had twisted his buttocks. I passed him, surrounded by my bodyguards, and he screamed at me, that

I thought I was a man just because I could buy the Igwe and the village and put them in my pocket but there was one thing I could never buy and that was my manhood.

This was the very point that the engine of my life knocked, just like that.

The silence that followed was the kind of silence that swallowed the village near Ubiaja when Chief Ato lifted up the head of the bat from his soup. I saw Barika's wife trying to cover his mouth but the demon of his anger gave him power to push the head nurse of Ikerre Health Centre, who was three times his size, to the ground.

He was shouting now: Leave me, let me talk! After all, if I am lying, let him pull down his trousers! Does he have what separates men from women? Then let him go and marry tomorrow like his mates! Look at him! And when they call for men he will stand up!

Even from the ground, his wife was pulling and pinching him, but it was too late, his anger had provoked him to say what they had been hiding for how many years now. Otherwise, how did Barika know the biggest secret in the Jumai family, if it wasn't that his wife was the very midwife that castrated me?

As for me, what did I say? I heard my voice sounding like an echo, saying that if he doubted my manhood he should bring along his daughter to my house; but it was foolish nonsense, the sort of stupid threat that you can hear from an angry man in a wheelchair.

It wasn't me that my bodyguards pushed into my car. It wasn't me that Nacet drove home. On the way, some boys saw my car and hailed me, *Ca-la-mi-ty!* That was when I knew what a terrible nickname I had. Were they referring to what had just happened in the Igwe's palace? Were they laughing at me? At home my boys kept whispering, the way that the whole Ikerre-Oti must be whispering right now, the way the whole of Delta State will be whispering by tomorrow: that no wonder he doesn't like women, that no wonder he's not married. The stump in my groin was burning. I wanted to do something terrible and final. I didn't want to cut and patch and wake up with a wound that was getting slightly better but would never totally heal.

I sat in the same place for three hours. See how my life has soured in one bite: I've chewed gall bladder in the middle of a mouthful of roasted goat. And the bitterness in my mouth has erased both the memory of old enjoyment and the prospect of future enjoyment.

The fax machines were singing and borning papers but they didn't move me to stand. Then Mangohead came in and began to read the faxes. I asked myself if I would take the shape of his head and his manhood if they were tied together in one parcel, and I couldn't even say Yes right away. Then he started jumping up and down, shouting: Hong Kong! Hong Kong! I looked at him as if *he* was crazy; and that was when I knew that there was a secret tumbler of madness deep inside everybody's brain, and that mine had cracked and was leaking psychosis.

I took the chair to Pa's grave and sat there for hours. He was blacker than I remembered him and he refused to use the second chair that my houseboys put beside the grave. This time I couldn't talk much; he was the one talking most of the talk. *Have you seen this life of a thing?* He kept repeating, *Have you seen why I shot him?*

You shouldn't have missed. I told him finally.

In the evening I sent Egbuna to buy me cartridges for the double barrel. The boy looked at me and began to shake. He begged me to forgive and forget, saying that if manhood was the problem, we should go to a doctor who could cut off his own and sew it on me, asking that he that had his manhood, what had he done with it? Then he saw my eyes and ran out of the house. One hour passed. When I didn't see him I sent Ode on the same errand.

Before Ode returned, Egbuna arrived with Chief Ato and Ugbaja. They begged me to forgive and forget, that everyone in Ikerre-Oti would happily trade their genitals — and two legs as well — for a fraction of my bank balance. They asked why I should allow one basket-mouth to spoil the enjoyment of my wealth — over something that happened more than twenty years ago... but when I looked at their faces I could see the pity inside their eyes; and that was when I knew that I had to pass through the door that Pa had opened.

Because there's nowhere that the fame of my wealth will reach that the shame of my wound won't reach as well. Because human ears prefer to hear bad news about other people. Now there's no woman who can look at me without that same pity in her eyes. And there's no man who can look at me without that pity. And the only thing I ever want to see in people's eyes is envy. And I'm not a child: I know that the distance between pity and contempt is like this. I can bear the private pain of my castration for one hundred years; but the public shame of it will kill me in one day. And there's no suffering in my past that will compare with the one waiting for me outside the gate of this compound: and there is no money that can cover it again. And if I run from this wicked village to the end of the world, eventually, I have to remove my clothes, and I cannot run from that!

By God! This is more than war! This is calamity!

They left in the night. On his way out, Ugbaja took my hand and said in a voice that was shaking like a woman's. Listen to me, he told me, you don't know how lucky you are. For me, every bad decision I've made in my life has been caused by my genitals.

But I knew that all the water in his eyes was caused by the smoke from the building contracts he could have got from me, which were burning up right in front of his eyes. By then Ode was back with the story that he found no cartridges to buy. Stupid fool. I locked the door and wrote a letter to Abel. I went to bed. Around 11 p.m. I woke up. How can everything end like this? I locked the door of my room. I opened all the cartons of cash. I poured them on the ground. I walked on the money. There was more paper money under my feet than in the whole of Ikerre-Oti. I was looking for a reason to continue, for the fire that licked my soul on the day I bathed with a bucket of wine. Instead I felt as if I was walking on dead leaves.

The fire was gone.

It was midnight. I was no longer ashamed to leave the compound. I can see now why Night is Shame's best friend. I went outside and drained some petrol from a car into a jerry can. My bodyguards were pretending to sleep. They were too afraid to wake up and confront me. I want to do something terrible and final. I don't want to cut and patch and wake up with a wound that is getting slightly better but will never heal. Back inside, I opened Pa's diary. I read his last page. What sort of life is this? By mistake, that witch conceived me in another man's bed. By mistake, my circumcision became a castration. By mistake, they called me Calamatus...

Tonight there'll be no mistake. And no sleep for the wicked either. If they like, they can run to the end of the world, I'm coming after them. This one isn't a matter of bullets finishing; I won't repeat Pa's mistake. My body can roast when I've finished, but before then I'll show some people that their past blunder wasn't an ordinary mistake.

It was a calamity.

DIARY THREE

ABEL MEME-JUMAI. (a.k.a. Anga Ali.)

Occupation:	**Writer.**
Last Known Address:	**Warri, Delta State, Nigeria.**
Date of Birth:	**December 25, 1973.**
Declared Wanted on:	**July 13, 2000**

ABEL

7th July 2000

WORST THING WAS HOW FATHER and son kept calling me 'jobless'. I'm a writer; that's what I am. — May not earn wages in cartons like conmen, but I have a profession. Pa farmed and Calama conned. I write; that is what I do. Why was that so difficult to understand? And frankly, if I don't have a regular job today, I've got Pa to thank for that. Because of him, I'm too big for the jobs I'm qualified for and unqualified for those I'm expected to do. Back in '94, when I wrote to tell him I was in jail in Cameroon, what did he do? Boasted to the whole of Ikerre-Oti that his first son had won a three-year scholarship to read Business Management in Cameroon University. Sneaked shamefully into the village after my '97 release, only to walk into a hero's welcome as the first Ikerre indigene to graduate with a first class honours degree.

Been living in fear of exposure ever since.

The car crash that broke Tendu's leg happened on the 4th of July. Got out of General Hospital today with a plaster-of-Paris cast on my elbow. Apparently that wasn't good enough for Tendu who has been threatening to break my own leg once he gets out of hospital. The car Calama loaned me was a write-off, and good riddance too.

Back home, a dirty paper-bag was waiting for me by the door to my room, along with four anxious notes from my mother.

Put three of the notes in the dustbin unread. — One of them had a newspaper cutting pinned to it that merited a glance. 'Vacancy: Trainee Manager. Qualifications: good BSc. Degree...' Tore it up and binned it. The paper-bag contained the diary started by Pa and continued by Calama, along with a letter from my brother advising his imminent suicide.

Had sworn *never* to phone him again. Yet, these circumstances were plainly extenuating. Went to a pay phone and called Calama's numbers. Rang on interminably. Tried the only other two telephones in Ikerre that I knew. Couldn't get the Igwe, but finally raised Johnny Bus-Stop's house. The one they called Nacet took the phone. Yes, the party was over. Calama was already dead. He'd flipped and gone on a manhunt like Pa.

He'd burnt down Barika's supermarket and died in the inferno. The Barikas were history, along with their merchandise. There was still a lot of confusion over what Calama did or didn't do. The morning after the fire, the wife of Etuk the bicycle-repairer was found in the old market with a stake through her heart. Etuk blamed Calama, but Ikerre hadn't been deaf to the recent quarrels between husband and wife. According to Nacet, Etuk had more in common with the dead than the living.

It was impossible to grieve for Calama.

After all, what did he do when he heard about my accident? Hospitalised from a motor accident and not a word of commiseration from your own brother. Plus, my room is empty now. Before he came meddling with his millions, Patie was living here. A wife was the one thing he could never have, and he resolutely destroyed it for me. Don't blame him too much though. Blame myself. — Acting like the family idiot instead of firstborn.

So the news from Ikerre drifted through my ears like rumours from another continent. Sat at my desk, with the diaries. Couldn't stop reading them once I started; read them straight through. Broke off several times though, to grind my teeth. It's one thing to know that your own blood despises you. It's another thing, a more vexing thing, to read their despising in the baldness of a rude diary.

Calama's handwriting is lousy. To worsen matters, he spells

things the way they sound, which is the way to get into trouble with a language like English. Sat there several hours. Found myself crossing 't's and dotting 'i's. It's a sickness I have. Crossing 't's and dotting 'i's that won't put a penny into the pocket. When I rose, it was still difficult to grieve for Pa or Calama.

But I'd started my own diary.

I'm the writer in this family, after all. Won't write a more interesting diary, that's for sure. They made their journals readable, Pa and Calama, by writing with their blood. Can see that now. Pa died at 50 and Calama at 25, the same fire consuming pauper-father and millionaire-son. Plan to live longer than both of them combined — and die in my bed.

Rather live a boring 80 years than write an interesting journal that ends in a blaze. Those four days in hospital gave me room to reflect. So let it be a boring diary, but I'm the writer in this family and I'll keep this tradition. Another generation of Jumai will read it; — and they'll know there's a difference between Jumai and Jumai.

I'll mention the centre of my life this once, and forget her. First time I was going to marry Patie, my father's reputation stood in the way. The second time, my brother's jealousy stood in the way. Won't be a third time. Had tried to mend fences after the bat incident. Stupid, stupid, *stupid*. Had gone to see her in the evening. Met her hanging clothes in her yard. She was smiling as I approached, smiling until she poured the bucket of dirty water all over me. Then she began to scream obscenities, the sort of things I never heard from her before.

That was the last exchange between us, a public airing of dirty linen. Realise now in retrospect, that the bat-wound was far too fresh... should have left reconciliation for five or six years hence. Can see now, from reading Pa's diary, the foolishness of having a wife whose leaving will fracture your sanity. Yes, I'm on fire now for Patie — and the son in her womb — but I'm not yet thirty.

The fire will die.

On the phone, Nacet had warned me to stay away from Ikerre-Oti — as it would be a shame for the same foot that broke the fowl's neck to crush her egg as well. Said Calama's suicide had cheated the villagers of their vengeance, and any Jumai who turned up within the next few months would inherit his lynching. — But I could hear the greed in his voice. If Calama's houseboys were keen to keep me from any part of my brother's inheritance, it certainly wasn't his lynching. The looting of Calama's property was obviously in progress.

Fools. As if I'd have waited for his death were I keen on his cash. There's a passion that fires me, and it's not just a passion for money. It is a passion for success, and inheriting from Calama doesn't qualify as success.

My passion is burning me up right now. Used to be desperate to write a successful book just to show all those who had given up on me. With the death of Pa and Calama, that list is getting shorter — and I'm getting more desperate.

Tendu's girlfriend, Sikira, came to see me today. Still lived with her parents three streets away, but already her stomach was bigger than Patie's. Only poverty had kept them from marriage. She opened Tendu's room, cleaned it as usual, and came and sat in mine; the way she'd sat by my bed in hospital. Her visits are thirty minutes long and designed to drive me crazy with guilt. All she weeps, over and over as she kneads her stomach, is: *So what are we going to do now?*

Never set out to live a false life, that's the truth. Got jailed and told Pa right away, but I returned to a stupendous reception hosted by the Igwe of Ikerre-Oti himself. To burst the community's delirious bubble at that party, that was beyond the willpower of any 24-year-old. Pa had deceived even my mother and my brother. At the welcome party, I was pushed to the microphone to make a speech. So what should I have told them? That I graduated from prison, not university?

Have never found a good moment, since then, to end the deception.

True, I envied Calamatus, but not the way he thought. Envied him for the honesty of his life. He was a conman and didn't hide it. Had the money to show for it too. I? Went to jail for a loaf. That's the truth. And never even got to eat the wretched bread. Now Pa who stuck me in this mess has died with his pride. I'm stuck with this permanent dread. It's not the prospect of an Ikerre lynching that I dread. It's the prospect of public exposure.

Ma came today again. Mine is the last in a bungalow of sixteen *face-me-I-face-you* rooms arranged down a dirty corridor. Heard her unsteady steps approaching in time to kill the radio. She knocked for five or six minutes before leaving on the heels she's taken to wearing since she resumed her 30-year-old liaison with the vulcaniser.

Despite what Pa preferred to believe, the vulcaniser's more businessman than workman. Owns garages in Warri, hasn't touched a tool in years, and is certainly not a roadside artisan. He's a dream Ma refused to wake up from.

From what I've gathered from a childhood of shouted quarrels, she was carrying on with him before she met Pa. If she can be believed, the whole relationship with Pa was designed to provoke the vulcaniser into jealousy. The strategy apparently backfired when I came along. Wasn't an ideal scenario to grow up in, but I could live with it... till the letter from her kitchen thatch turned up.

After she left, it took me another thirty minutes to get back to work, and when I did, I wrote nonsense for hours. Wasn't all down to Ma's visit though. It's getting more and more difficult to be a writer with Aboye living next door. He's a member of my Old Boy's Club. (Stumbled on the Old Boys Club by accident, this informal band of ex-cons who had done time in Bamenda. Strange how most of the money I've made from writing has come from the political fiction I've done for Old Boys...) Aboye never knew his father but his mother was Urhobo, and that was good enough for him. Last week the perennial conflict between the Urhobo and Itsekiri ethnic groups flared again and Aboye led some Urhobo misfits in the razing of several Itsekiri houses.

He graduated from Bamenda prison in the same year that I did. He'd done six years for violence occasioning harm. He's still occasioning harm three years afterwards. There are many of us Bamenda Old Boys in Warri. Left prison planning to close that chapter of my life, but had gained a certain reputation because of a petition I wrote to the Commandant. There'd been a riot in the prison over poor food. Got out of hand. Dozen prisoners and wardens were hospitalised, five convicts got their prison terms doubled. Then I wrote the petition and got forty convicts to sign on. The petition brought out the Prisons Commandant on an inspection, three officers were sacked and our meals improved.

Only lasted a few days, but it was long enough to earn me a reputation. Guess that's what went to my head, gave me the idea I could live on my writing.

There's talk of reprisals from Itsekiri vigilantes. Newspapers are ominous. Only today, *The Herald* reported a police seizure of a cache of firebombs in the boot of a car heading from Sapele to Warri. It's getting harder to write about the travails of an urbane tortoise when restive tribal zealots can firebomb you at any moment.

Come night, lay on the bed a long time. Still extremely difficult to grieve for Calama. Yet... my goodness. *My brother was dead.*

8th July 2000

HAD THE BEST GCE in Ikerre-Oti, back in '94, but could Pa sponsor me through University? No. Passed the matriculation exams and went off to read History. Struggled through the first term before being kicked out with unpaid bills. And what was Pa's response? Apprenticed me to Sammy Plug at the Trailer Park, collecting fifty naira a week for my services. My job was to race alongside motorists with a fistful of spark plugs. After two weeks and uncountable fifty-metre dashes, I'd sold only sixteen plugs. Did the numbers: After my apprenticeship, as a Spark Plug Trader, I'd have to sell thirty plugs a day to eat three square meals. So I abandoned my apprenticeship and crossed the border into Cameroon. All that is history now...

Newspapers sold out this morning. Brutal headlines: the assassination of an Urhobo state commissioner. The killer had stepped out of a car in full Itsekiri regalia complete with feathered cap. Town's divided already, with many Urhobo wives not talking with Itsekiri husbands. Personally, I smell a rat. There are more practical outfits, even for Itsekiri assassins, than ceremonial regalia.

Went out early today, despite my strong resolve not to. Was hanging around in the crowded Elumelu bus stop at 7.30 am when she arrived to open up her shop. Almost fell down when I saw her silhouette. Wasn't quite flat, but there was no child in there anymore, that's for certain. My son was either born or dead. Slipped away before she spotted me.

Was washing clothes in the yard when Sikira came this morning. Sight of a man washing clothes with one hand in p.o.p. calls for some sympathy. All Sikira did was cross her hands over her stomach and ask tearfully: *So what are we going to do now?*

These people won't drive me crazy.

Went into the room and filled a shopping bag with some money from Calama's carton. Don't think Patie will ever come back anyway, if the birth or miscarriage of our child doesn't bring her back. Called Sikira in and told her what we were going to do now: gave her the bag. Told her to keep it safe till Tendu got out of hospital. Would help him set up a provision store since his scaffolding-climbing days were over. She left without a word. Pushed the depleted carton back under the bed.

Wondered if my son was dead or alive, if she'd have called him Ezra as we planned.

There was a letter for me in the post with the logo of Eterna Publishers on the envelope. I've had five rejections from them thus far, but they still have two of my manuscripts under consideration. To extend that dreamlike time during which I was a potentially published writer, I left the letter unopened on Pa's diary and went to the bathroom. I play such harmless games with hope.

Ma visited again this morning. Caught me with a bucket of water on my way to the communal bathroom across the yard. Too late to dodge. Greeted her coolly. She raised a rumpus over the p.o.p. on my elbow but I played it down, told her I slipped in the bathroom the day before. She was dressed in damask, the sort she never wore in all our years in Pa's house. As usual, the eyebrows she had drawn over her eyes were unequal. She was carrying a flask of food for me. Told her Patie was out, surrendered my room key and went on to the bathroom.

Minutes into my bath, remembered something and aborted it. Hurried back to my room with ears and armpits full of suds. Too late. She was sitting by my writing desk, reading Pa's diary, which I'd left open at yesterday's date.

I stood dripping water at the entrance to my room.

The braids in her hair were swaying, exaggerating the movement of her head. She had dished my yam pottage. Her bag and its contents were spread over my bed. She'd drawn my curtains apart, opened my window and changed my radio to her choice of channels. She looked up from the page. Her chin was shaking, *You? You went* to *jail in* '94?

She had read the first paragraph. Dripped some more water as I steeled myself to snatch the book. It was too late. She raised a thunderstruck face to me. You didn't read my letters? *You threw them away?*

There was nothing to say. Every time I meet Ma I become fourteen years again. There's something wrong with me. That's what it is. With her I'm incapable of the routine rudeness that even teenagers practice without qualms. That's the root of this nonsense about me loving her. One of the characters I met in Bamenda was in jail for killing his mother. Me? I can't even talk back to mine.

She flipped to the very first page of Pa's diary and read some more. Under the damask, her legs were shaking. By the third page she showed that she might be hurt and wounded, but her name was still Stella Jumai. At 48, there were two things no one could take away from her: first, her beauty; second, her ferocity.

Remembered Calama's appendix operation of '89, but not the way Pa remembered it. Calama was dying on the floor and Pa was just muttering: *What sort of world is this now?* Ma didn't have the deposit for the hospital either, but she left the house screaming at the top of her voice and before she got to the end of the street, she had the deposit in her hand. She ripped a handful of pages from the diary, balled them up and flung them at me. The rest of the book fell to the ground and she jumped on it. She kicked a leg from under my desk, spilling my files across the room. She was shouting, cursing Pa for poisoning my mind against her.

On the corridor, doors began to fly open. Had never entertained in the compound, wasn't going to start now. Stepped fully into the room and shut the door — just as Aboye's head poked out of his room next door. Pulled on a crumpled pair of trousers under my towel, zipped up and stripped off the towel. She was cursing Pa as usual with death by motor accident. Realized, with shock, that the thousands of curses she had sown into Pa had germinated, and she hadn't even heard of the catastrophic harvest. Drew on a vest, as a tightness across my chest seemed to snap and something like a cork jumped out of my mouth. Your prayers have been answered. I said.

She stopped abruptly. What's that?

The devil joined together all your curses and added pepper. I told her, carefully replacing the leg of my desk. Since my tenancy started weeks ago, it had given way twice. First time was right after the bat-head episode when Patie's brother came to take her travelling bag. If it happens a third time I'll replace the desk. I stood up and faced her. I needed to see her eyes. Pa died last month. I told her. The villagers burned him alive.

Ma became extremely quiet. She looked away and sat down suddenly. The new voice that came out of her was sober, shaky and belonged to a human being. She begged me to tell her I was joking. I picked up the crumpled pages and straightened them out. What was that Calama wrote about 'killing' and 'talking about killing'. Two different countries, I think he'd called them. Pa had dreamt of driving a car only so as to drop a tip on the ground for the man that stole this woman. Now, she slapped herself viciously and grabbed her left breast. Knowing her, I recognized that she was close to tears. Truth about Ma was that no one who knew her fury could doubt the genuineness of her grief either.

And I won't take it, I swear it, for her to weep for Pa in this very room. Heart pounded at the confrontation ahead. Straightened up the squeezed-up pages, put the punished diary back into her hands again. Knowing what her husband and son thought of her might spare me some crocodile tears. Ma's mourning skills were respected in Ikerre-Oti. No matter how wicked the deceased, if the immediate family had the good sense to invite Ma to weep at his graveside, only someone whose heart was carved from ironwood could leave with dry eyes.

She was making tragic noises as she read the diary of a man she deserted not quite six weeks ago; so I went and closed the window. Tried to reassemble the pages of my manuscripts scattered all over the floor. She flipped rapidly through the diary. She was normally a very slow reader. Clearly she was barely reading, probably still digesting the news I'd given her.

Doesn't know about Calama yet. He's her real favourite, although he had no time for her. People talk about Ma and I as if there's a special relationship between us. Remember very well how it all started: two days that changed our relationship completely.

First day was ten years ago. Returned from school with a headache. Caught her in the kitchen with the Birom man that hawked *suya* in the Village Square. Before that day she used to treat me like the person who ruined her destiny with the vulcaniser. Didn't report her to Pa; and she's never abused me since then.

Second day was when I came back from prison. Probably thought that my first class degree would change her name from Mrs. Sufferhead, the number of job adverts she's brought me over the years. So I know what her 'love' is about: my silence, — and the diploma I don't even have.

She reached the last page of Pa's diary. She broke off her low-key wail and grabbed me: What happened? I looked at her. Real or fake, her tears had ruined her makeup. Hardest thing for me was to see my mother, real and actual wife of a farmer, losing her eyebrows at age forty-eight.

She'd lost the pencilled brows again with all the weeping. Told her how Pa killed three men and was burnt alive in the Square. She screamed and rose in slow motion. Her hands stretched towards the ceiling, as if the fire that consumed Pa was burning again. The diary and her shawl fell on the ground.

Decided to get everything over at once. Told her how Calama was also dead. Only thing I hate more than a soap opera is a rerun of a soap opera. She screamed and started whooping, ducking her head like a fowl. Would have been comical, but this was my family. One minute of that, and she slapped me twice and asked what happened to her son. Couldn't be offended because all this while she was boxing herself insane. Told her that Calama had discovered the identity of the careless midwife, and that her entire household was burnt beyond hope of recognition. Told her never to return to Ikerre-Oti if she didn't want to be lynched in his place. She began to whoop again, making little jumps in the air, turning around in a small circle.

Opened my wardrobe for a shirt, but stood there several minutes after I chose one, unable to turn around. Although I didn't weep when I heard of Pa and Calama's deaths, my eyes were filling up now. Now understand how a professional mourner can provoke people to tears at the funerals of perfect strangers: the mourner's grief, whether real or fake, can jump intellect and ignite emotion. It's like watching a yawn. It's impossible to be critical about Ma's emotions. Whether she was raging or grieving, her passions were too raw and elemental for objectivity. They provoked reaction.

That was what happened to me as I faced that wardrobe, and it was the beginning of that hypocrisy that finally strengthened me to confront and break with Ma. It wasn't the logic of her self-centred life. It was the fear that I'd become like her, weeping for a man I loathed, a man whom I'd turn away from, should he walk into the room that minute. Turned to her. Realized at that moment that my days of sonship were over.

It's time for you to go. I said. Didn't shout, but the sense of my words cut through the racket of her moans.

What did you say?

I've seen your letter to your Honey-Joe, I told her hoarsely. The one you wrote in '74, the one you hid in the kitchen roof.

What letter?

12 January 1974, I began, quoting from an etched memory. Couldn't help the bitter sarcasm in my voice: *My dearest Honey-Joe, Why are you doing me like this now? Upon all the letters that I write to you, why can't you reply even one line.*

Tha's enough.

If you hear that Stella has died, you shouldn't just sorry at all because is you that has killed me.

I said tha's enough! She shrilled.

I paused. Took a deep breath and spoke quietly, quoting the end of the letter: *But if you prefer us to start again from the start, me I don't mind, Honey-Joe, is you I want. I can leave the farmer with his bastard even this tomorrow, just give me eye, that's all.*

My mother continued to weep. She had that talent, even when she was cheating Pa, to weep with such sincerity that when the peacemaker arrived he took a look at Pa's stony face and gave all his sympathy to Ma. This time, I steeled myself as she took my hand.

My baby... you're not a...

Don't repeat that word. I warned her. Bury all of us today. From now on, face your new family.

You're my blood, Abi, my only blood.

You've made your choice, Ma. You wanted the clothes and the money.

Don't know what I expected, but the prospect of the loss of her 'only blood' didn't provoke another round of dramatics. Instead she smiled slowly through her tears. She sat down and ran her fingers slowly down the damask that clothed her laps. There was a placid complacence in her that told me that my break with her would never rank, for her, as tragedy. She'd arrived at that station in life where my silence concerning her indiscretion was irrelevant, where my future prospects were irrelevant to hers.

You forgot already! She shook her head, *Banza!* Thirty years of *story-story.* Meme sucked me dry, can't you see my breasts like slippers? I remember how I use to dress like house-girl, how I was dry like stockfish, how I will manage one pot of soup for two weeks until it was tasting like mud peppersoup. She smiled. Just see me now, Abi, dressing like human being again! See my cheeks, see my shoes! Don't you want good things for your own mother?

Said nothing, just stared at her, but my eyes must have been response enough, because she suddenly flared. Okay, if I wrote the letter, so therefore? Attimes you check the pieces of your life and say mistake to this one... mistake to that one...

Yes, I snapped, without thinking, but my children will never be mistakes, they'll never be bastards.

Okay, she fumed, so you're a bastard? So therefore? Am I not a bastard myself? The baby that Patie girl is carrying for you, isn't it a bastard?

Terrible silence in the room. The woman's brutal tongue was at the root of my ambivalent feelings for her. My loathing for Pa came from his living with her for all the years it took for her tongue to cut him to bits. Finally, I broke the silence, grasping at some substance. Who was my real father?

She sulked. How should I know, when I was drunk that night? Something that happened so many years ago.

My hands were shaking. Did not believe I was having this conversation with my mother. Was it Meme Jumai?

She laughed incredulously.

Was it... I almost gagged... the vulcaniser?

Her eyebrows puckered in thought, then she saw my face and her eyes seemed to glaze over. What does it matter? Something that happened thirty years ago?

I think it is better for you to go now. I said finally.

She flinched. Her lips inched up. If I made you a bastard is it also my fault that you're an ex-convict as well? She rose arrogantly. Look at the wretched room you're driving me from! Go and look at a mirror! How somebody can resemble a man that didn't even father him is what I don't know.

She picked up her bag and began, determinedly to paint a face on. Stood there, waiting for her to leave. Head was buzzing. Heart was pounding. This was a scene I had played in my mind hundreds of times. Wasn't working the way I planned. Wasn't coming out looking as good as I'd thought.

Abi? she said, snapping shut her compact case. Her eyebrows were back on. Her smile was threatening.

Yes Ma.

You're driving me from your house?

Yes Ma.

You know what happened to your brother and your father?

I said nothing.

Tha's mercy-killing! She cursed bitterly, her face as hard as her voice, Tha's mercy-killing, compared to what will happen to you. See, she pushed out the tip of her tongue, tha's what said it.

Then she rose and left.

My mother left.

Bolted the door. Was shaking as I straightened up the room. Put her food in the bin. Didn't know what to do with her flask. Was near to tears — and very cross with myself. Calama was right. I was soft in the head. Had suffered her indifference and abuses, but was unprepared for her curses... Then I realised it wasn't the curse that unsettled me. In a sense I'd just buried my mother. Won't see her again, even if she predeceased me. I stopped kicking myself then, I'd earned the right to spill some emotion.

Rediscovered the mail from Eterna Publishers as I straightened up my room. Opened it. It was an invitation to a meeting with the publisher! My exhilaration penetrated the numbness from my mother's visit. They still had two manuscripts of mine. They were my best work yet, *The Beasts of Wrath* and *The Dilemma of a Tortoise.* Was I looking at a double-book contract?

Had started writing when I got chucked out of University. My last assignment was a five-page term paper on *A History of my Hometown.* My vacation stretched out and so did the term paper. It's now three hundred pages long. — I turned up the weirdest things about Ikerre-Oti, which spun my term paper off into new directions. It's now called *A History of the Slaving Kings.* It's heavy-going now, this history: no written sources... unreliable legends... I'll probably be eighty before it's finished.

I'd continued writing in prison. Learnt fiction by lying about what put me in jail. Developed my lexis and structure from writing petitions for other cons. The prison library had a few dozen books, when I finished reading the interesting ones, I started writing mine. Same sort of challenge that provoked me into this diary. Finished my first manuscript five years ago but have never received a letter from a publisher that didn't start: Regretfully...

Until today.

Didn't sleep much tonight either. Lay in the darkness with the letter from Eterna on my chest. Still difficult to grieve. But the news in the letter was crying to be shared. And... *Calama was dead.*

9th July 2000

TENDU GOT OUT OF HOSPITAL this morning. His left leg had been removed from the knee. Was ashamed of the wheelchair and refused to leave the compound. Sat there in the yard from morning to night, cursing me every time I came into sight, telling commiserators how I crashed the car in broad daylight just to kill him.

There's nothing much wrong with my elbow, that's the truth. The x-rays were fine and the doctor was confused, but I screamed every time someone touched it. The p.o.p. was my idea. Needed something to help me look Tendu in the eye.

Still can't look Tendu in the eye.

This world is a terrible place. Particularly for someone who can only *think* about his problems and not *talk* to anyone. Wasn't trying to kill him, of course. Was trying to kill myself. Didn't plan a suicide, or anything like that, am not crazy or something.

Was just a grenade of self-disgust that exploded inside me at one-twenty kilometres-per-hour along the Warri-Sapele Expressway. Blew me off the rail for the critical second. Swerved the car into the pole. Was it really Tendu sitting there beside me? When my mind blew, for that critical second, thought it was Stella Honey-Joe...

Running away to Cameroon was the worst thing I ever did with my life. Family friends, the Momodus, lived in the capital, Yaounde. Their letters had been friendly from afar but they were downright nasty when I turned up on their doorstep. Slept in a bus station that night. Next day, spent my last coins over a lunch counter. Couldn't even get a runner's job at the spare parts market.

Heard things were better in Bamenda and hitched a ride there. Got a job at a carwash during the day, slept in an empty car during the night. My boss wouldn't pay an advance. Had enough time to regret fleeing from Pa and Sammy Plug. My second day without food and I had that problem with the supermarket loaf. They called it shoplifting and put me away for three years.

Didn't need to worry about food or shelter for a while.

Discovered a pecking order in prison with murderers at the top and petty thieves right at the bottom. Owning up to stealing a loaf of bread could have literally killed me. Posed as a big-time cheque forger. Had to invent new incidents from my career every time a gossip session got underway. Fault of mine: among the respectable I'm ashamed to be an ex-con but among convicts, I hankered for respect as well. Was ignored in prison until November '96 when I wrote that petition. Earned the dignified alias, "The Forge".

It was easy for me to choose writing as a career: only respectable profession open to a man with an invisible first class degree in Business Management. Unfortunately, my career isn't yet off the ground. All the things I've published I'm ashamed of, and all the things I'm proud of, I haven't published. Safe to say that I'd have starved, but for the patronage of the Old Boys Club...

Why won't publishers take a chance on me? Must everybody write like Chinua Achebe? I like to write about Tortoises. That is how I am.

Tezera is publisher of Eterna House. He started shouting at me as soon as I walked through the door. At first I thought I'd entered the wrong office, but he was shouting about my manuscripts. Said a folktale was a folktale and a novel was a novel. Asked what one had to do with the other. Said I was driving his readers nuts with my scripts. Asked why I needed one hundred and fifty thousand words to tell a folktale about Tortoise and his brother-in-law, Chameleon.

He was screaming: Enough! Enough! Enough! As though I was hard of hearing. He was panting when he eventually sat down.

Stood near the door as I explained quietly to him that I'd had more than five years' exposure in the genre and that from my experience when folktales grew up they all wanted to be novels.

Had never seen a character as emotional as Tezera. He was a squat bald man whose head was corrugated into ridges that flowed into the muscular neck of a labourer. He was pounding his desk as he spoke.

Any bystander would have assumed there was a personal quarrel between us. He asked what made me think that one hundred million years of evolution would bring Tortoise, even in the realms of fantasy or science fiction, to drive an internal combustion engine, use aftershave lotion, marry across species *and* address a political rally.

His secretary brought him a file, which he flung across the office at a coffee table already sagging with the weight of dog-eared manuscripts, cursing that this was the consequence of free speech: that if I had to buy words by the dozen I wouldn't write such rot.

Inched closer to the door as I tried to reason with him. Told him that the incident of Tortoise applying cologne before addressing a local government congress was towards the end of my manuscript and if he'd read that far, he ought to confess that my stories were interesting.

He came round his desk gesticulating violently, but no longer as loud as before. Got more worried as he came within punching distance. — But he only continued to talk: Said that asking whether I had talent was like asking whether elephants had ears. Said that all the ears in the world wouldn't help elephants fly, and that everything had its proper place. Said he'd read my stories through, stubbornly, to discover whether my madness had any boundaries at all.

He began to count off his fingers: said he was rejecting my Tortoise story, my Skunk story, my Monkey story and my Boa Constrictor story. Said he couldn't stop me sending manuscripts to his office, but that if I sent him any other story in which any character had both a tail and the power of speech, he'd consider it a personal insult.

He was calming down now. Gave me one of his 'successful' books, *Midnight Darkness* by Abim Khan, which was now reprinted every two to three months. He said Khan was now the owner of several cars purchased from royalties, and booksellers often came to blows in his warehouse over copies of *Midnight Darkness*. As he was seeing me off, he smiled for the first time and seemed to become another human being.

He advised me to do something about my name. Said, from his experience, that a writer's success started from the very sound of his name, whereas my middle name sounded like the bleating of a goat with a stammer. He patted my shoulder when I said nothing. He was sweating on his nose and in his armpits. And he was still panting.

Thought to myself that if this publisher expended so much energy on scripts he did not like, he was well on the way to a coronary.

He said he liked how I took constructive criticism, adding that he'd meant to come down really hard on me but had pulled his punches because of my broken arm.

That was when he asked something peculiar: Jumai... That's not a common name... are you the same Jumai that spent time in Cameroon?

Stood there moping. My surprise had no near relations. This was a publisher I was trusting to carry me into respectability. He had no business knowing about my Cameroon chapter. I managed to shrug meaninglessly, which seemed to satisfy him, and he asked me to see him at noon, day after next, with the outline for a decent book.

Got home from that meeting before noon; was dazed for hours. Threw *Midnight Darkness* behind my book pile. Sat down at my desk. Couldn't write. Couldn't eat either. The numbness from Ma's visit was settling back in with a vengeance.

Three weeks earlier, an old pensioner from Upper Caulcrick Street had knocked on my door to ask if I was the writer they said lived at No. 61. He wanted a letter written to his nephew who worked in a hotel in Kafanchan. Told him I wasn't that kind of writer. He was a difficult man. Said English had only one alphabet and either a man could write it or he couldn't. Left my door grumbling about illiterates posing as graduates.

Stubborn questions harassed me: Was I wasting my life? What was my business with the matrimonial relations of tortoises and chameleons anyway — or their political affiliations for that matter? Was my destiny mired in the squalor of gossip columns and the infamy of political fiction? Her food flask was red, that was part of the problem. Every time I looked up it caught my eye. Took it to the dustbin outside.

No good. Still kept thinking about her.

Went to the offices of *The Probe*. Even among gossip newspapers, *The Probe* was a disgrace. I give them articles under the penname, Anga Ali. I also write about animals here: the editor will print stories of beastly behaviour — so long as a celebrity was involved.

The editor, Ebenezer, was an Old Boy who was jailed for an editorial indiscretion in his native Cameroon. He had an assignment for me. He also did agency work for political parties and wanted me to tag along to a UPP rally at Okari the next day to file a pro-UPP report. The genre of political fiction is a demanding one. It wasn't just a matter of slanting reports; often it was a matter of *creating* reports favourable to the client. Ebenezer focused on my elbow and frowned. Told him I was a writer not a boxer and he left me the brief.

Returned home to Caulcrick Street. The tenants were yakking in the yard. Overheard the Isoko man and the Kalabari woman discussing me. The Isoko man thought I should pay Tendu's rent for at least one year. The Kalabari woman thought all the tenants of No. 61 should take a collection to help Tendu sue the pants off me. They were not embarrassed when they noticed I was back, but eventually they changed the subject of their gossip to Aboye, the loose cannon next door. Sat in the darkness of my room, listening to my neighbours' voices.

Aboye styles himself an Urhobo freedom fighter, but he's more of a political tout really, making most of his money in the run-ups to election when his talents were most in demand. It's one thing for me to want to put my prison past behind me, but if he hadn't recognized me the day I was negotiating with the caretaker, I might still be house-hunting now. The caretaker had told me there were a couple of people ahead of me in line for the room, but when Aboye stepped in, the queue disappeared. Later, Aboye had taken me along to a clandestine meeting of a cell of the Old Boy's Club where I picked up several political fiction assignments.

Yet, he was six feet six inches tall, kept home-made bombs under his bed, and deployed handshakes that could occasion harm. Although his room was adjacent to mine, I contrived to keep severely to myself.

There's a lot of tension concerning the Itsekiri's imminent strike and my cotenants haven't improved things, the way they've carried on. To make sure revenging Itsekiris didn't pillage the wrong apartment, they'd painted their tribal identities on their doors. I read 'Kalabari Tenant', 'Yoruba Tenant', 'Isoko Tenant', and 'Itsekiri Tenant' all the way down the corridor to my room. Even Aboye had taken liberties with his ancestry, painting 'Hausa Tenant' on his own door.

Only mine remained unmarked. What do I write, after all? Ma's father was a fly-by-night tanker driver who didn't disclose his ethnic identity before abandoning his Edo hostess with an unpaid bill. Pa was mostly Hausa, but that was neither here nor there, because my biological father was a mystery. So my door stayed dangerously plain; and I had every reason for nervousness.

10th July 2000

A DIARY'S A USEFUL THING, for ferreting the secret thoughts of men. So Calama thought me a snake and Pa had cause to wish me dead? No surprise there. He must have known he was my father only in name. Only physical contact he had with me throughout my childhood was the sting of his cane.

The UPP campaign bus was due to pick me up at 6 am, but there was some excitement at 5 am. Was roused by anxious knocking on the door. For some reason, I imagined it was Patie. Opened door for Aboye who slipped in and dived wordlessly past me. Was barely awake, and the speed with which he disappeared under my bed caused me to wonder momentarily, whether I was still dreaming.

Heard yells from the end of the corridor and had the good sense to shut and bolt my door. Went back to bed, but of course there was no chance of sleep. A riot swept the corridor. Listened to the breathing of the giant under my bed as his room next door was broken into and trashed, Hausa notice notwithstanding.

An hour passed, the Itsekiri war cries receded and when we heard the police sirens it was obvious that the storm had passed. Calama's carton preceded Aboye out from under my bed. He emerged with his mouth open. He had a bundle of currency one hand and the diary (which I had taken to hiding under the bed since the fiasco with my mother) in the other hand. Slow poison! He exclaimed, No wonder they're asking questions about you! What's your racket?

Answered very coolly. Didn't fancy 'Slow Poison' for a nickname, and the reputation for keeping cartons of currency under my bed wasn't one that could assure my longevity. It's not mine. I told him. I'm keeping it for somebody.

Didn't have too much in common with Aboye. He was a man dominated by his physical attributes, His voice was a foghorn base and his conversations had the robustness of public announcements. Now he was suddenly chummier than I remembered him as I pried the money from his hand and pushed the carton back under the bed. You have to pack out of this area if you want to live long, I told him as I led him out to assess the damage to his room. But I knew that now that he had discovered the money, I ought to take my own advice.

Within fifteen minutes, the UPP campaign bus arrived. Tendu was already in the corridor when we passed and he grabbed me. With one hand in p.o.p, I could barely defend myself and he had torn my clothes and my notebooks before Aboye rescued me. Entered the bus shaken; had arrived at Okari before I got Tendu's spittle out of my ear.

The bus made several other stops for staff before leaving for Ikerre North. The assassination of the Rep for Ikerre North has opened the evenly split House of Assembly once again and the two parties were treating this by-election like a presidential campaign. A six billion-naira State Budget Appropriation Bill was currently deadlocked at the House of Assembly. First official act of the winner of the by-election would be to break that deadlock. That was several billion naira too much resting on one by-election.

Today's campaign started in Okari, thirty kilometres north of Ikerre-Oti and swung through six towns and villages. The UPP candidate was an Old Boy, Adoja Moto: handsome lawyer, rich family, and one skeleton in his cupboard, twelve months in the Bamenda slammer for indecent assault fifteen years ago. He was charismatic and well spoken, but it didn't help him in Okari, where they booed everything he said. Ikerre North was a stronghold of his opponent, Chief Orinso, the GNP candidate.

The rallies were a flop. Apart from our rented crowd, two hundred or so people attended the six rallies, although many of them showed their affiliations by defying Aboye's team and singing GNP's campaign songs.

The drive back to Warri took less than an hour but by the time we arrived, I had finished my article on the rallies. Gave it to Ebenezer's protocol officer in exchange for an envelope of money. Felt like a prostitute as I did so, but the fact is, political work was cash-on-delivery. Got off the bus at the beginning of Caulcrick Street. Aboye had dropped off earlier to drink with his team. Walked soberly home. Tendu was in the corridor so I entered through the back door. Dozed till 5 pm.

Was roused by shrieking. Got out into the passage to see a clump of people around the door to Tendu's room. Didn't venture too close, but Aboye suddenly appeared behind me and forced his way in. For his size, he was a lover of gossip. He later came back with the story: After spending hours daily with him in hospital, Sikira hadn't been to see Tendu at all since he was discharged. A worried Tendu had sent a boy to Sikira that afternoon to make sure she was well.

The boy had found the home of Sikira's parents repainted and refurnished. Sikira herself had relocated to Lagos, leaving a letter for Tendu. He'd started shrieking after reading it.

Was a struggle to do yesterday's diary entry. Don't know how long I can keep this up. Depressed. Just sitting here, staring at my finished and unfinished manuscripts. How much better than Calama was I then, messing up the matrimonial lives of others. Clearly, poverty and sudden wealth didn't mix well. Or perhaps Billy Barber had put a powerful curse on his money.

So what am I going to do now?

Have been unable to shake the depression I acquired in Tezera's office. — Or the one I acquired in Ubiaja. — Or the one I acquired from Stella Honey-Joe. In the blackness of my mood there was only one pinprick of light: Tezera had conceded that I had some talent. However grumpily he'd put it, he'd found my writing interesting. A publisher didn't have to fib. It was now a simple matter of writing the books he liked or getting him to like the books I wrote. All he wanted from me by next day was the outline for a "decent book" he could publish.

Decided this evening to see if there was anything else, besides okra, in the pot of soup: started reading Tezera's bestseller. Title: *Midnight Darkness.* Wonder what else one should expect at midnight other than darkness. God will help us. Opened it.

The armed robbery started in the first paragraph of the first page of chapter one. Fifteen men with pistols and rifles and pick-axes. Imagine this sort of nonsense. I was 17 years old before I witnessed my first armed robbery and here was a fifteen-man affair, right in the first line of Tezera's bestseller. Continued to read. Suppose this kung fu expert is our hero. His name? Randy. On that, I'll make no comments at all. Randy was in the bank to cash a cheque but by paragraph five, between his kung fu and a metal chair, he had knocked all fifteen robbers unconscious by hitting them once on the head.

Now, I am 27 years old and in my personal experience when you hit a man on the head, if he doesn't die he makes you regret the day you were born. He doesn't fall asleep until the police arrive.

And here's the sort of nonsense Tezera wants me to write. Continued to read. There was a girl in the bank with her life savings. Naturally she was both beautiful and marriageable. Our man Randy saves not only her life but her wealth as well. Naturally, she's grateful and by page three she's proving it... and this is the sort of idiocy Tezera wants from me?

So am I a prostitute or what? In the daytime I'll write trash for Ebenezer as Anga Ali and in the night I'll write trash for Tezera as Abel Randy. If my Tortoise tales are far-fetched, what was the word for *Midnight Darkness*? If this is what it means to be a writer then I'd rather get a messenger job like my grandfather.

Clearly, if mother hen forsook her crowing she'd have nothing else to raise her chicks by: everyone to his own lunacy. I stopped reading and tossed the book into the bin. Then I remembered something and retrieved it. Checked the last page.

After three hundred and sixty pages, of course Randy and the rich and beautiful girl are to be married. Is that not "living happily ever after" then? What's the difference between this fairy tale and my folk tales? Suddenly found myself shredding the book. Was panting like Tezera when I was through.

Had a strange visitor in the evening. It was one of Calama's boys, Ode. Seems he was the one that brought the diaries to my house. In his new suit he looked more businessman than houseboy. Recognized him right away, although I didn't immediately recall his name.

Asked him his business. Seems he merely came to update me on my brother's affairs. Didn't recollect requesting an update — but the talkative person misses his turn at the kola bowl. Held my peace. He said he was representing my brother's apprentices. Seems they had formed a cooperative venture, which they called The Calama Group. He said that while my brother had made me next-of-kin in one of his Warri accounts, The Calama Group had vested interests in the money as well. He suggested that since they knew about the account and I didn't, we could do a fifty-fifty split.

Told him I wasn't interested.

He smiled and said he wasn't talking about thousands of naira but tens of millions of naira.

Told him that even if he was talking about hundreds of billions of naira I still wasn't interested. He didn't say another word until I let him out of my room. Suppose he was still stunned, because minutes passed and I didn't hear him walking away from my door. Eventually he knocked again. When I opened the door a second time, he was sounding more like houseboy than businessman.

It was the same oily sycophancy of the hooligans that surrounded my brother in his last days. If it was the matter of my brother's other properties, he was saying, I shouldn't be annoyed. It was the greedy people of Ikerre-Oti who looted the house. I shouldn't imagine that Calama's loyal houseboys were responsible, because they themselves had to flee for their own lives to avoid the fury of the wretched Ikerre people.

I assured him that I had other personal reasons not to want to inherit from my brother.

He paused and then changed tack painfully. If it was the matter of the percentage, he told me, at a pinch, he could persuade the other members of The Calama Group to consider a 60:40 split in my favour — but that was absolutely his best offer.

Told him my decision would not be different even if the split was 90:10 in my favour. Once again, I witnessed the transformation of Ode from solicitous houseboy to thwarted businessman. The features of his face resolved from grin to glare. You want it all for yourself, don't you? He snarled, Mister Hundred Percent! You think you can find it yourself, eh? Well, I was lying, I knew you were going to double-cross us, the bank is not in Warri. It's not in Sapele, it's not even in Asaba, without us you will never find it.

His angry footsteps faded into silence. Wondered fleetingly if Calama had actually appointed a snake for his next-of-kin. More likely, his boys were now rehearsing some of his cons on me. Obviously they hadn't forgotten the carton of currency they had put in my boot not a dozen days earlier. I felt a little insulted by all that. Surely they should expect the children of the household to recognise who was wearing the masquerade.

ABEL

11th July 2000

ABOYE BROUGHT ME A COPY of *The Probe* this morning. Told me he could throw Tendu down the well in the yard if the cripple was harassing me too much. Wasn't sure if he was joking or serious. Didn't try to find out. Shut the door. My article on the UPP rally made the front page. Didn't want to think what Adoja Moto had paid for that. Ebenezer had found a file picture of an ecstatic crowd scene to support the banner headline: *UPP in Sell-out Rallies.* My seven-hundred-word essay reported the largest rallies in Delta State in years. Voters had carried Adoja Moto shoulder-high at the end of each of the six rallies. Attendance estimates ran into several thousands...

Couldn't finish the article. Stayed in bed for years. Reread Pa's diary. Can feel a major depression coming. Was I any different from him then? With a by-line in hack-journalism and a room full of rejection slips, my harvest was every inch as rotten as his. And for all the posturing, my political fiction was sounding just as bad as Calama's cons. What was the big difference between Dr. Amechi and Anga Ali?

Yet, I had an opportunity to put Anga Ali behind me. Got out a pad and tried to write an outline for Tezera. Had to get my mind out of the animal world. Think human. Think formula. Had to put something powerful in the first paragraph. War, Earthquake, Flood... Had to get a young man for a hero... Put a young woman in the picture...

As I worked, I felt a permanent sneer contorting my face. When I put down my pen two hours later, the bin was full of balled-up papers, but I had an outline that Anga Ali would have been proud of. Doesn't matter if I'm ashamed of it.

Half-an-hour to my appointment with Tezera; after our first meeting it was difficult to be enthusiastic about a second meeting with the publisher. It was desperation that drove me to the gates of Eterna House.

The Secretary announced "the Tortoise man" on her intercom but the great man kept me waiting for an hour-and-a-half before he asked me in. When I finally entered his office I was surprised to find half the sofa occupied by a gross man in flamboyant three-piece suit. He was taller than he was fat, but only just: occupied the sofa with all the permanence of something installed by forklift.

From the letterhead of Eterna Publishers I knew that Chief Martin Orinso, whose praise name was 'Eagle that flies without perching' was a director of the company. What I hadn't expected was to see him in Tezera's office with my manuscripts before him. On the coffee table beside the mound of scripts was a bundle of newspaper cuttings. On top of it lay the latest issue of *The Probe,* which was lying open, with my article face up. My throat dried up.

Sit down Abel, said Tezera, surely you're not allergic to politicians?

Maybe he is, wheezed Chief Orinso, you know how much tortoises dislike eagles.

As they laughed, I discovered that Tezera's laughter was just as uncontrollable as his anger. I sat. Being the butt of their joke, I felt no obligation to join in. Perhaps for that reason, Tezera, when he quietened down, indulged a spot of flattery.

I like you. Tezera decided, Despite your silly stories, you actually know how to use English Language. You have a gift for bringing characters to life with two sentences. He paused. Although all the characterisation in the world won't make me want to read your political thrillers if your hero is a mouse!

He stood up and walked to a shelf. Take this book for instance, he continued, pulling out a volume. It was *Madness Unlimited,* by his favourite writer. Abim knows how to keep a tale spinning, but his manuscripts have to spend months with a university lecturer before they're ready for typesetting.

I don't want a university lecturer. Warned Chief Orinso.

Forget university lecturers, replied Tezera grandly, I give you Abel Meme-Jumai.

Meme-Jumai, what sort of name is that? It will look funny on my book.

He's about to change it, said Tezera.

Oh no he's not. The large man swivelled towards me. That was the same name you used in your letter-writing days in prison, wasn't it?

When I continued to stare at him, he explained. My intelligence people were digging up the dirt on the so-called Mr. Anga Ali when they discovered you — and somebody who knew you better as 'The Forge'. But you can relax. He gestured at *The Probe*. Despite this, you'll find that you are among friends.

I didn't speak. Suddenly the world seemed full of ex-convicts. My self-esteem was never lower than at that moment. The greatest desire of my life had been a brand new life as a writer, yet, the only commissions I got seemed to emanate from my prison connections. To cap it all, I finally got a meeting with a big-time publisher; and not only were they unimpressed by my present work, their interest in me appeared firmly rooted in my prison past.

I've read the fiction you write for the whores at UPP, continued Chief Orinso. He had an earnest voice, too highly pitched for his physique. It was possible to take him seriously by focusing away from his comic body, at the intense oval face that stared at me. And I have read your moralizing manuscripts, which tell me that righteousness is a two hundred and seventh bone in your body. He paused. I have one question for you. What is UPP paying you to sell your soul to the devil?

I shrugged, loathing a sermon from someone of Chief Orinso's moral stature. Or his ancestry. The name Orinso wasn't new to me. It was the subject of two dozen pages of my research notes for my old term-paper. His village, Ikerre-Ntefe was sixty kilometres south of Ikerre-Oti. He was the son of Minas Orinso, who was the son of Emerson Orinso, son of Mathias Orinso, grandson of Crema Orinso, son of Monos Orinso, son of Iga Orinso, who was either the son or Grandson of Rugato Orinso, who in his time was the most powerful slave dealer between Benin and the Delta.

Chief Orinso rarely addressed rallies. His regular campaign strategy was to identify hostile precincts and buy and restuff their ballot boxes. The significance of this by-election however had redoubled security. He was going to have to devise a new strategy.

He chuckled: I understand, the answer might incriminate you. Listen, I have a simple deal for you, but it requires a serious commitment, which means backing away from the goons at UPP, — and stabbing them in the back. But it will make you a famous multimillionaire. He chuckled again. Is that a sacrifice you can handle?

I continued to stare at him.

He paused. When he turned to Tezera there was some irritation in his voice: You didn't tell me he had a problem with his tongue.

I thought I was here to discuss improvements to *The Dilemma of a Tortoise.* I said, disgusted by the whine in my own voice.

You'd better sort out your own dilemma first. Said Tezera severely.

I have the authority of my board of directors, said Chief Orinso pompously, to offer you a two-book-contract. He tried to stifle a belch and failed. He drained a remedial glass of squash before he continued, What concerns me is the first book, which you will write to order for me. It must be ready in time for the elections next month. I can't promise you that the second book will sell, particularly if you insist on writing about lizards and tortoises, but as for the first, I can tell you now that we will distribute half a million copies to voters in this state and you will be paid royalties for every single one.

Chief Orinso leaned across, provoking complaints from the

sofa. He pulled an untidy folder of handwritten notes, press cuttings and photocopied letters from a textile bag and pushed them across the coffee table towards me. On top of it were several bundles of well-used naira notes. You're going to do a quality hatchet job on Adoja before the next election and I'm going to make it a bestseller. I want to be in print before Election Day. I've written the title, you'll write the rest.

You're asking me to betray Adoja Moto...

I'm asking you to be true to yourself. Think like a writer, not a faithful lap dog. What would Adoja have done in your shoes? Tezera says you've sent us seven manuscripts so far. At an average of a hundred and fifty thousand words, that is over a million words in the dustbin of Eterna Publishers alone. I am asking you to decide between being a failure for the rest of your life and becoming a successful, published author.

What's the title? I asked.

Adoja Moto, Artful Dodger.

Three weeks?

I'll check you into a room in my Pegasus Hotel. Said Chief Orinso. You won't have to cook or work. You'll just eat and write and sleep and write. The research has been done for you and you have the imagination of a storyteller. You can do the fifty thousand words in two weeks.

They'll kill me.

That's every rich man's fear, said Tezera patronizingly, but it's no reason to embrace poverty.

What are your chances of getting a fifty-thousand-naira book advance within the next one year? Asked Chief Orinso.

Zero, said Tezera cheerfully. He nodded at *The Probe*. And I know what Ebenezer pays for a cover story. He lowered his voice. Comes a time in the life of every man when he's got to decide whether he can pay the price of success. Abel, this is the first and only time in your life that a real publisher will offer you a two-book deal. If I were you, I'd jump.

There was silence in the room, then Chief Orinso said intensely, Book one guarantees you blanket name-recognition. You'll be famous in half the state and notorious in the other half. That guarantees the sale of all your other books. He paused and lowered his voice: And listen, I've got Tezera to promise me this, he'll publish any second manuscript you deliver. He grinned. How's that?

I said nothing immediately. I already knew one manuscript they would not publish in a million years. In what I had written of *The Slaving Kings* thus far, I'd concluded that the original Ikerre-Oti had been decimated and her survivors exiled by too close a proximity to the slave-raiders of Rugato Orinso. Finally, I cleared my throat. You want me to ghostwrite your book?

He laughed cynically. Anga Ali strikes again! You think I'm going to pay a fifty-thousand-naira advance to a ghost? Forget it, you're going to get your real name dirty this time. But don't worry, Nelson Mandela was also a jailbird, and look what he went on to become... Anga Ali is dead anyway, if you leave here without a deal with me, my own newspapers will discredit *The Probe's* cover story by linking Anga Ali with Abel Meme-Jumai and The Forge. — And I'm sure you can tell your jail story more compassionately than my own hatchet men.

At this point, I left to use the toilet. When I returned, I still hadn't reached a decision. I'll have to sleep over this, I told them eventually.

This particular opportunity knocks only once. Said Chief Orinso tersely; I have no room for indecisive tortoises in my team. When I make a marriage proposal, a 'Maybe' is equal to a 'No'.

Why me? I asked eventually.

Chief Orinso leaned forward, pushing his fat fingers deep into a bowl of groundnuts. As he ate, pieces fell on his jacket and were brushed onto the ground. Unlike you, he explained, Adoja Moto went to jail under a false name. There's no document to prove his jail term. He gestured at *The Probe*. People are now too sophisticated for an article like this. If we expose him in one of my papers, it will be discounted as political mudslinging. But not if a former associate of his, a professional writer and fellow jailbird does a serious biography claiming that Adoja Moto served six years for rape in his cell block!

Twelve months.

What?

He served twelve months for indecent assault, not six years for rape.

You'll say six years for rape, grinned Chief Orinso. I dare him to publish a correction. Once your book is out, I'll launch the final leg of my campaign. I'll serialise the book in every paper in the state. In those last days before the by-election, if Adoja shows his face in public or at any rally, he'll be mobbed. He refilled his glass and took a long sip from it, watching me carefully. If you write the book, next month I'll be a member of the house. You will have a friend in high places.

Three books. I said eventually.

Sorry?

I want a contract for two more books after *Artful Dodger*. In writing.

Done. Said the Chief without so much as a glance in Tezera's direction. He smiled when I leaned forward to take the folders and the money. Not so fast, come in this time tomorrow for your written contract. *Then* you'll have your money.

Despite the murkiness of my three-book-deal, there was a discernible buoyancy in my mood when I left Eterna Publishers. Impossible to be rational about things like that. After five years of yearning, with a publishing contract only 24 hours away, it was difficult to stay depressed. Until I got home.

Found my door ajar. Doorknob was swinging by a single screw and my bed was standing on its side. The room had been thoroughly ransacked, it was as though a storm had swept the room. Perhaps the only things I had of value to a petty thief were the transistor and electric fan that Pa had thought were his. They were still there, but my manuscripts, bags and clothes were strewn all over the place. Once again, the dodgy leg had given way: if the desk fell a fourth time I would really have to throw it out. My room had been burgled in broad daylight, but my neighbours saw and heard nothing.

Postman joined me at the door. He brought a letter from Rajan Community Bank. Its customer, Calamatus Jumai, had recently passed on. As next-of-kin, could I take steps to file for probate in order to put his bank balance under administration?

Stared at the letter for ages. Ode had been telling the truth after all! The bank had stipulated no figures. Went back to the diary, read up the last few days of Calama's life. Hard to translate FazO's 'huge sums' or Mangohead's 'Hong Kong! Hong Kong!' into coherent figures...

If this was how breakthroughs came, in a flurry of three-book-deals, burglaries that cost me nothing and multi-million naira inheritances, then they were worth waiting for, after all.

Aboye came back home an hour after I fixed the door. He wasn't as chummy as he had been that morning. Wondered if I was supposed to apologise for hiding away the carton of cash. Had seen the armed robber in him climb out from under my bed; the difficulty of pulling the bundle of currency from his fingers had finally decided me.

Had been ambiguous about Calama's money, but once Aboye had seen it, all I had to do to lose it was nothing. And, poverty's a terrible thing. Between a private nest egg under the bed and the faintest possibility that Patie would walk in through the door, I had come down hard on the side of pragmatism. Had transferred the contents of the carton into a dirty bag, which I stowed overnight in the broken freezer in the yard.

Don't much like the trappings of wealth. The excessive pomp of the second Ubiaja marriage embarrassed me no end, even before the catastrophe that ended it. But there's a door that opened in my mind as I read the letter from Rajan. Liberated massive delusions of grandeur, that's what it did. Many times a day I see myself flourishing a signature on a white marble counter in a banking hall.

Of course I won't dress in flashy colours, just a sober grey. And there will be no loud convoy, just a compact BMW... The letter from the bank had not specified a figure. But Ode had mentioned tens of millions. That kind of money was an excellent accompaniment to publishing success, and could cure any variety of insanity. Hard to believe that Calama could have flipped with that kind of money in the bank.

Had another late night visitor. It was Egbuna, another of Calama's houseboys. He was as well-dressed as Ode before him. Told me that he had sworn an oath to my brother, which obligated him to tell me something. I told him to put his conscience at ease and he told of a conspiracy he knew of, whose object was my death. I asked him who the conspirators were — and what object my death would serve them — and he got angry. He said this was what came of too much education. That instead of accepting the hooting of an owl as a universal omen of death, I was trying to cross-examine the owl.

I waited for the catch and it came: he gave me a card. Said to call him if for any reason I needed a large sum of money to disappear with. I nodded. Put the card in the bin as soon as he left the room.

When the bungalow quietened down, I rose and walked to the toilet end. Once there, turned into the mini scrap yard that had developed in the nether areas of the yard. There, negotiating the carcass of a wardrobe and a tower of bald tyres, I put my hand into the darkness of the broken freezer, Calama's money was there alright. Went back into my room, went to bed and tried to sleep.

Not much chance for that. Came back to earth slowly but firmly. Orinso had agreed to a three-book deal without so much as a glance at Tezera who was after all, the Publisher. They hadn't considered the deal; did they intend to honour it? Were they leading me down the garden path just to get me to put out *Artful Dodger*? Tezera hadn't asked to see the outline. Hardly credible that the same man who loathed my folktales two days ago would suddenly write two blank cheques to publish anything I wrote.

Besides, from my perspective, what was the point of a three-book deal if I'd only live to write the first one? Betraying Aboye's Old Boy's Club was only conceivable when combined with a life in a distant exile.

Between my shaky three-book deal, the imminent reprisal of the Itsekiris and Egbuna's vague warning, didn't sleep much tonight. The sixteen households in the bungalow had shrunk to nine, but I had nowhere to run. Several times during the night I stepped out to use the toilet. Am beginning to loath night times. Spent much of this one thinking about Pa. He was twenty-nine in my earliest memories of him and he was grey-haired even then. Don't remember ever seeing him laugh either. He told the occasional joke, I remember strained smiles — but I don't remember his laughter.

Hit me suddenly at 2 am. Don't remember mine either.

ABEL

12th July 2000

5 AM, AND I WAS wide-awake. Life was getting, overall, far too interesting for my liking. Game plan of a boring life that went on and on seems to have derailed at some point. There was some confusion in the neighbourhood. Two streets away, the house of an Urhobo pensioner was burning. Heard the commotion and went to look-see.

Owner of the house was a seventy-year-old retired teacher who did nothing all day except read newspapers from cover to cover. Had leapt from the balcony to the garage roof, and thence to safety, but as his house burnt he sat in the centre of the road and refused to budge.

By the time I returned to my room, the panic had spread. Aboye went underground again, and many tenants of 61 Caulcrick were packing up and moving out to relations. The fat Isoko man in room 5 tried to reassure us: he had requested police protection and there was no need to flee.

If so, asked the carwash attendant in room 7, where's your wife and daughters?

Turned out they were visiting cousins in far away Ibusa. The panic escalated. By dawn, only five rooms in No 61 remained occupied and mine was one of them. Was given credit for more courage than I had. Truth was, had nowhere to go. Added insomnia to my woes that night. Was well past dawn before I managed to sleep.

Woke tenish. There was a banging on my door. Opened the door for the most expensive suit I ever saw. The man wearing it didn't look like a pauper either. Stood there, groggy, as he walked into the dishevelled room. The man was walking on manuscripts and looked a little stunned by his surroundings.

You must be Abel, he was saying. His smile was patronising and dogged; I was looking at a man determined to be amiable.

And you are?

FazO, he said, drawing out the 'O'. He tried to sit on my table as if he was a film star or something and he fell down with it. Decided finally to throw away the table.

Recognised his name straightaway from Calama's diary. Also had a fair idea what he wanted. He picked himself up from the ground carefully. Suit was unmarked, elbow seemed sore, but his ego was deeply wounded: he seemed to take falling down very personal. Insisted we talk in his car. I supposed he was uncomfortable in my room.

Felt uncomfortable as well, when I saw the limosine outside, particularly with Tendu cursing behind me. FazO talked and I listened. His speech was mostly puff and conceit. As we crawled around the streets of Warri in the black monstrosity, he pointed out to me the buildings that belonged to him or his syndicate. He told me how my brother was one of his most promising boys and how he wanted to invite me to take his place in the business.

By this time, an hour had passed. Was surly with sleeplessness. Realised, at that pace, that our talk would take all day. Asked him if he wanted back the money he put in my brother's account.

He was silent for a long time. I believe it was at that definitive point that the tension between us soured into antipathy. It was curious that a man who was such a good friend of my brother could become so malevolent towards me... on second thoughts, it wasn't so curious after all.

So you know about that? He asked.

Continued to stare at him quietly.

Yes. He said finally. Yes, that's what I want. The smile that shrunk after his fall in the room had finally disappeared. The embarrassment of being caught out had scuttled his amity.

Why do you need me? You're chairman of the bank.

He faltered, then he snapped. Don't talk like a child. This is a bank, not a village association; a chairman can't just put his hand in the vault and take money, even if it belongs to him.

How much is your money?

He didn't bat an eyelid as he said, Everything in his account is mine.

I supposed, in a sense, that it was. After all, he'd taught Calama all he knew about fraud. How much was it? I persisted.

He flared unexpectedly, Isn't it rude to ask people the contents of their own wallets? This is not a matter of 'how much'. Just come along with me and sign some papers...

I'm going to have to sleep over this...

To sleep over what? Another person's money?

No, I have to sleep over *my signature*. — Besides, I'm busy today.

There was a tense silence, then he snarled. I can see that madness runs in your blood. His eyes were ominous slits. Look! He dug his index and middle fingers under his eyes, You see these eyes? They've seen every kind of madness that money can cause. He raised his hands. They were carrying six or seven kilograms of precious metals and stones. You see these hands? They have cured them all. See this big car? He waved a hand, taking in the cavernous interior, It isn't big enough to hold the corpses of those who have salivated for my money.

Got the point; but in between being henpecked by Orinso and heckled by FazO, I cracked. The driver slowed down to negotiate a turn and I pushed the door open and jumped onto the street. Slammed the door and stalked the five streets back to my room.

Tendu was cursing as I came through the doors of the bungalow; tried to grab me as I passed. Furiously, I yanked his chair around, spilling him on the ground and kicking his hands away. It was the surprise of my retaliation more than anything that bested him, for even without a leg, he was a very well-built man. As I jumped past him for my room, the curses of the neighbours who only saw an able-bodied man kicking a cripple followed me till I slammed my door behind the world.

Made Eterna House just before 3 pm. They didn't keep me waiting this time. Tezera seemed preoccupied and was in and out of the office all the time. Orinso was as immobile as ever on the sofa. There were printed contracts laid out on the coffee table. Picked up a set. The small print was eight pages long, but they were printed forms, didn't seem to have been drafted just for me. The written-in bits seemed okay too; *The Artful Dodger* was to be delivered three weeks from date. Two further books were to be delivered within two years from date. A royalty advance of fifty thousand naira was payable on date, royalties of 10% of net receipts were payable, to be charged against the royalty advance.

I signed two copies and pushed them across to Chief Orinso who paused and dusted off the fragments of tea biscuits on his fingers. Instead of reaching for a pen, he pushed across another stack of papers to me. They are related forms. He explained, turning back to his tea.

I picked up the papers and straightaway felt the blood drain from my face. The name Rajan Community Bank jumped at me. Rested my hands on the coffee table to hide their trembling. Chief Orinso was speaking. Fabian Malite Eze tells me you're sitting on my campaign funds.

Fabian Malite Eze?

FazO to you. He's a GNP caucus treasurer. Used to be Chairman of Rajan Community Bank till the Central Bank shake-up, a couple of weeks ago.

Didn't trust myself to speak.

You know of course that politics is all about fundraising, Chief Orinso continued, FazO's antecedents are rather... he made an iffy, gesture with his fingers, ...but he has decent political instincts and has been treasurer of one of our state caucuses for six years now. I'm told that my campaign funds were transferred in error to your late brother's account. He produced a pen. All you have to do is sign these forms to retransfer them.

Took the pen. Swallowed. Looked down at the form. Tezera came in, hurrying towards his desk. He paused beside the coffee table when he saw the forms before me. A word jumped into my mind, unbidden, from Calama's lexicon: *mugu*. There was a singing in my ears and bile in my tongue. Could feel my shoulders slump as I dropped in stature from potential author to real-time *mugu*.

These gaps. I asked hoarsely, how much is the money, whose account is it being transferred into...?

Just sign it, Chief Orinso snapped, these are bank forms and neither of us are bankers. It's a banking error and you can't keep this money.

I don't like signing blank sheets of paper, I said quietly.

You're messing with your future, Chief Orinso said menacingly, This is your three-book-deal you're playing with.

You're messing with your royalties, added Tezera. His mouth twitched. He seemed about to explode into one of his fits of disproportionate rage. You're tying up the funds for the publication of *Adoja Moto; Artful Dodger.*

Felt a rush of despair. My mind backtracked, sieving furiously through the garbage I'd been fed in this office over the past few days. Tried to sort truth from deception, then the reality hit me with concussive force. There was nothing to sort! It was one seamless tapestry of manipulative lies!

I was no master of the English Language! My two sentences didn't bring characters to life! There was no three-book-deal waiting to catapult me into the rarefied world of the successful published writer! If I delivered a manuscript for *The Artful Dodger* it would more likely be fed to a shredder than a press!

Had been thinking like a character in an Abim Khan novel. It wasn't going to be "happy ever after". Delta State elections were not won by circulating knocked-up biographies by Abel

Meme-Jumai. They were won by deploying chests of cash. I might be in the presence of a future Member of Parliament, but I was also in the lair of practised conmen. Was caught in an elaborate intrigue whose object was my signature on documents that would divest me of Calama's bank balance. Began to lose my hearing as usual. There are blood vessels in my ear canal, I think, that are engorged by fear. Repeated numbly: I don't like signing blank sheets of paper.

Could see Chief Orinso's mouth moving. Thought he looked furious from his nose upward, and comical between bellows-like cheeks and jowls. Turned and walked away.

Interesting how Pa died in a fire and Calama died in a fire and now I'm to die in a fire as well. Borrowed a brazier at home and set it up in the yard. Moved my washing out of the drift of smoke, got my manuscripts out and burned everything. Works in progress, duplicates, germs, everything. Burned Tortoise and Boa Constrictor. Burned the damned Chameleon. Burned *Monkey's Tale*, burned *What the Eagle Saw*, burned the four revisions of *A History of the Slaving Kings* and my portmanteau of notes — and the experimental *Tales of an Itinerant Slug.* Was weeping as I burned everything. Neighbours' kids came out to give a hand. So much glee while I burned. Glee in their voices and tears on their cheeks. Was a game for them. For me, it wasn't just the smoke that brought the tears. It was the self-immolation. I mourned my dreams, my genre, I mourned myself.

13th July 2000

WOKE UP TO THE SOUND of knocking. Remained on the bed for several seconds, trying to calm a rampaging heart. Who's there? I demanded.

Me, came Tendu's voice. Wasn't quite 6 am. Nerves were jangling as I rose, but something in his voice told me I wasn't going to hear much abuse that morning. Opened the door cautiously and he rolled in. A smell of sewers hit me. His eyes were slits, but they were swollen, red slits. He rolled swiftly across the room, lurched out of the chair and onto my bed. Hoisted himself up till he was propped against the wall, the way he had spent many evenings when his legs were whole. His chin was set and trembling.

I can't kill myself, Abel; you've got to help me.

His abuses had distracted me from the obvious exigencies of his life. He was a building-site carpenter who spent all his time building roofs and scaffolding. Like me, he was in the market for a new career. And wife. And child.

His nearest relative was a sister who retailed pepper in five naira pans in a Sapele night market. His rent would run out in two weeks and he was a very short crawl away from the beggars' queue at the Post Office. His one-liner provoked more guilt in me than all the abuses he had spat my way over the past few days. It's not that bad, I lied, bending over to fold away his chair.

I tried to push myself into the well. He choked, I couldn't.

He looked drawn and haggard. You haven't been eating? I asked.

I haven't been able to eat since Sikira left. I even got myself a gun... but I can't... He gripped my arm viciously. You crashed that car because of Patie, not so? You're the only one who can understand how it is. Help me do it...

Tried to be casual as I pried my p.o.p. free. I don't know about you, I said, trying for flippancy, but dying requires plenty of strength.

Hauled up the wheelchair and wrestled it to the top of my wardrobe. With one arm in p.o.p. Had to recruit the wall to my aid. Can't be many neighbours still asleep after that, but at least, he wasn't going to run away and do anything rash until I returned. Let me see if the *akara* woman has woken up.

I slipped out of the room.

The *akara* woman on Caulcrick Street had woken up, but only just, and the fire under her pan was not yet burning. Would be another thirty minutes before her oil was hot enough for frying. Had to walk four streets to find one with *akara* balls already frying in oil. Bought enough to feed two hungry canoeists embarking on a marathon voyage from life to death.

Yet, didn't need the food as much as I needed the space to think. Had too much depression inside me to counsel anyone, I thought. No, it wasn't because of Patie, it was because of Stella Honey-Joe. And no, suicide was no more an option for me. I had burned my dreams already, now I was going to wring out every boring day of my life.

Decided to take another risk. I'd give Tendu the balance of Calama's money. Perhaps that would turn him from the certainties of death to the vague possibilities of life. The *akara* balls were burning hot and I was tossing them from hand-to-hand as I hurried home. Surely it wasn't possible for anyone with this kind of fire in his stomach to contemplate suicide.

Entered No. 61. Realised that the corridor was unnaturally crowded for the time of morning. More curiously, I could see faces from No. 59, No. 63 and further afield. My first thought was that at last, they'd got Aboye. Then I saw the giant look back towards me over the heads of the other neighbours. There was some bemusement, and a certain pity, in his face.

Then cries of 'That's him!' arose and the crowd parted as I pressed through. Aboye's room was shut, mine was open. Was still carrying the oily wrap of bean cakes. Dropped it when I saw the blood. Staggered into my room. His wheelchair was still on top of my wardrobe and he was still on my bed. Nothing else was the same.

Blood was everywhere, and still oozing from his head. Stupendous, the volume of blood two small holes in his head had spewed all over my bed and floor. Bullet had gone straight through. His brains spattered the wall. People were cursing and heaving around me. My neighbours' vomit was sticky on the threshold. A gut-wrenching stench filled the air. Couldn't think. As usual, my hearing conked out immediately. Gradually realised that my neighbours' voices were aggressive, not commiserative. Then a hand grabbed my good arm and hauled me backwards, down the short length of the corridor, and into the yard.

Foolish boy, he whispered in his foghorn, I told you to leave it to me.

What? What?

Why so stupid? In your own room! Now there's going to be trouble, they've called the police.

Was silent. Could hear my heart pounding. Grabbed his shirt and whispered savagely. I didn't do anything; I just went to buy *akara* and came back to meet this...

Akara! For you and your worst enemy? At six o'clock in the morning? Aboye shook his head disgustedly; You should have left this thing for experts.

Could hear the sound of sirens approaching. Looked despairingly into the clearing sky. Could already see the sceptical eyes of police interrogators, looking from my prison record to the cash in the freezer, from a hundred vengeful testimonies of Tendu's accusations to the inexplicable millions waiting in the bank for me. Over their shoulders I could see the malevolent eyes of Chief Orinso and his cohort, FazO, looking for an aperture through which to accelerate a life sentence with a single bullet.

Aboye shook his head with the air of an expert. The Forge, he murmured, let me tell you, this is worse than Bamenda. You're looking at firing squad O, if they don't lynch you first.

Whirled around. Some of my washing was still on the clothesline. Snapped three off the line and balled them up. Turned to Aboye. Didn't know what I was going to do, but I knew what I couldn't do. The notebook on my desk, can you bring it out for me?

Notebook? He stared at me as though I was crazy, but he returned into the house. Swiftly, I threaded my way through the junk in the corner of the yard, lifted the top of the disused freezer and hauled out the bag. Was stuffing clean clothes down it when Aboye came out. Put the diary in and zipped it up. Looked up at Aboye. Thanks, Old Boy.

Run as far as possible, he advised. Don't stop at Cameroon. Go to Gabon, go to Congo. Go. Go. *Go!*

Then he helped me over the wall.

Have made it as far as the motor park. Have some thirty minutes to finish this entry before disappearing for good. Pa, now this is how to die like a lizard: to expire alone on the road between somewhere and nowhere, perishing without a marker for your grave. Ma, don't know what the future holds, but if this is you at work, you curse like a witch, you know. Doesn't look like I'll be a success after all. All I can hope now is to break the curse of the Jumai, grow old without incident, and be interred without immolation.

Now I am a fugitive from justice, and from whoever murdered poor Tendu, thinking he was me. Unless he was killed, thinking he was Aboye. Or unless he killed himself, thinking to punish me by hanging his homicide on me. Can see the rest of my squalid life stretch out. Am probably the richest fugitive Ikerre-Oti will ever spawn, but the price of coming into Calama's inheritance won't merely be assassination at FazO's hands, but certain prosecution for a murder I didn't commit. Can pay neither price. Am on a one-way road into a great silence.

But I can't disappear without a cry. Have to appoint a next-of kin myself.

Who will have these diaries? Could keep them of course, yet a bequest is evidence of life, a scratch on the surface of existence. Won't disappear without a ripple. *If Ezra lives!* He was eight months in the womb when the bat-head thing happened. Perhaps he was born and not miscarried. If Ezra lives, it will be a lifetime of a maligned paternity. He'll someday want to read our version. Bus is revving up now. My fellow passengers are also clearly suicidal. Bus is a forty-seater modified to carry sixty, built with a welding gun from six or seven scrapyard carcasses... but it was travelling the farthest from Warri, and I have paid the fare.

Have stamped an envelope. Have addressed it, front and back — hesitated over a sender's address, then used the Ikerre-Oti house. Have another few minutes for an appeal to Patie to execute my will.

The dead may bequeath, the living will re-bequeath. In the end, life boils down to the Please.

Will sign the last entry of this diary with the flourish I'd thought to use in the banking hall, on the day I came into an inheritance too stunning for FazO or Chief Orinso to put a figure to. There comes a day in your life when you recognise that Opportunity may be knocking his knuckles numb, but it's no business of yours.

He wasn't knocking for your father. He wasn't knocking for your brother. And he definitely isn't knocking for you.

23rd November, 2001

WAS A MEETING CLEARLY SCHEDULED from hell itself: Billy Barber and the wrong Jumai.

Returned home to Ikerre-Oti after a fifteen-month self-imposed exile. Expected to have to fight for Pa's compound, like my brother before me. Surprised to find both Pa's house and the burnt-out shell of Calama's house deserted. The so-called Calama-Group had disbanded.

And they weren't even sacked by the villagers.

Ma-Caro had described how, soon after I fled Warri, a quarrel over spoils had escalated into the conflagration — and a bloodbath of houseboys. Two of Calama's boys were dead, three more were maimed, and the villagers were satisfied that the Jumai compound was jinxed, too dangerous, even for use as a rubbish dump. If the villagers evinced any interest in me, it was a morbid waiting to see what fiery fate would overtake me.

Was no good at writing fiction any longer. Every time I picked up a pen I was overwhelmed by visions of manuscripts burning in the yard of 61 Caulcrick Street. Even diary entries were beyond me.

(Had found the diaries in the postbox's pile of dusty letters. It was still in my envelope. Sealed. I'd recognised Patie's 'R.T.S.' right away: her brief, eloquent epitaph on the stone of our relationship.)

Several times since my return the month before, I'd tried to resume the daily record of what was now a satisfactorily boring existence. Yet, that memory of burning papers in the yard always cured me.

Until tonight. Tonight, I think I can write forever. Heard a banging on my door, above Ma'Caro's noisy haggling with her goat-seller. Went to investigate. Opened the door for a tall, heavy man with jet-black moustache and grinding teeth. He wore a heavy overcoat and his frame blocked out the yellow light from the yard. His eyes were dark and implacable. His hands were deep within his pockets, and he had a thin smile that never really left his face — even when he advised me of my imminent death.

I am Billy Barber, he told me in a deep, singsong voice whose morphing vowels swallowed their consonants and made him out a foreigner. When my mouth dropped open his smile widened and he pushed me back inside the house. Yeah, he said with satisfaction, I knew you'd remember the name.

Next door, a goat began to bleat as Ma'Caro led it to the slab.

Yes, it was a meeting definitely conceived in hell itself. Billy Barber and the wrong Jumai. Spent all of two hours trying to persuade him I was the wrong brother. But he had the mental incontinence and one-track mind of an ex-con just released from prison. He had served only one of a three-year term, but twelve months of good-behaviour that had earned him early release was a small price to pay for one final act of bad behaviour. He didn't care if he was executed, so long as I preceded him to hell. He'd proved his determination too: despite Calama's conspiracy with the man from the phone company, he'd contrived to trace the fax numbers of 'Dr. Amechi' and 'Inspector Tijani' right up to the Jumai Compound.

I sat him across the table from me; same table I used for interviewing oral history sources for my book. From the street, the house still appeared dilapidated, but once inside, I'd furnished it pretty comfortably. Offered him a drink which he brushed aside impatiently. Told him I was Abel Jumai, and the person he was wanting was Calamatus Jumai.

He told me I could be Abel, Amechi, Tijuana or Clementine.

Said I was free to die under any alias I chose.

I explained that I knew his name — and had reacted to it — because of my familiarity with my brother's diary. Even tried to get him to read some of Calama's entries in the diary.

He pushed away the book furiously: You must be a stark raving lunatic, if you're still trying to con me!

My ear canals began to bung up. My mouth dried up. Drier than months ago when I first saw Tendu's corpse. Drier than weeks ago when I was caught up in a bread riot in Chad Republic, with bloody machetes flailing in my face.

My brother's dead now, I told him, but some of your money might still be in his bank, we can try...

He laughed without mirth, giving me my third close-up of a handgun. He told me that if there was one thing he owed me, it was thanks for how I'd killed his greed quite dead. Told me he'd lost his wife, his job and his life; plus he, Billy Barber, now had a prison record. Told me that if he had a million dollars he'd pay it gladly for the privilege of strangling me.

But I tell you, I'm the wrong Jumai!

Really? He asked, clenching down a yawn, So what's your job, Mr. Wrong Jumai? How do you pay your bills?

I hesitated. I'm not a conman. I assured him.

Yeah? I've been watching this house day and night for two days. Yesterday I was at the bar next door from morning till they closed down. You didn't step out once. All you did was entertain old men from morning to night. Tell me, what's your latest scam?

I'm no scammer. I was researching a book. It's called *A History of the Slaving Kings...*

Indeed! You're not a farmer. You don't have a job. But look at this!

We both looked silently around the well-appointed room. I swallowed.

I... I'm a writer. I confessed.

Yeah? He grinned. Show me one book. Just one book with

your name on it.

I took a deep breath. I'm not published yet.

His grin widened. So, Mr. Wrong Jumai hasn't published yet — although he gets huge royalty advances seeing as how he hails from Chinua Achebe's village, yeah? Fine, show me one letter from a publisher. Go on, open your files. One royalty check.

I shook my head.

Mr. Wronged Conman, he said. His smile was very thin indeed. If this is the house of a writer, where's your typewriter? Your computer? Show me *one* unpublished manuscript.

I... destroyed all my scripts, many months ago.

He lost his temper. But you're researching a book you said! Only yesterday you were interviewing old men, have you forgotten? Where are your research notes? Where are the first *ten* pages of your new book?

Just now, I said quietly, I have a problem with writing. I make all my notes on tape.

I rose to get my tape-recorder as he flipped and slammed his weapon down on the table. There was an explosive discharge, the gun whirred around, and a hole appeared in the rear of a sofa three feet from me. I dropped back into my chair, shaken. He appeared more surprised than I, but recovered his bitterness pretty quickly. I waited for the villagers to come running to my rescue, but all I heard after the sharp report was the bleating of a nervous goat.

He looked at me for a long time then he said with depth of feeling. You're a pathetic liar. You're going to meet your maker in a few minutes and you can't even find it in you to say the truth and clear your conscience.

I'm telling the truth, I whispered.

I don't know how an incompetent clown like you could have fooled me in a million years.

That hour passed. Heard Ma'Caro's boys arrive next door. The goat died in a swift altercation of oaths and desperate bleats. I grew hoarse and fell silent. The voices next door receded as they withdrew into the kitchen. Still can't believe my neighbour would hear the discharge of an assassin's firearm — and continue to dice the goat meat for tomorrow's soup. Billy Barber took his turn to fill Ikerre's cowardly silence. Seemed as though his need to talk was at least as urgent as his need for revenge.

He sat there, significantly overweight, in the same room in which Meme Jumai had starved, moaning to a survivor of four years of Camerounian incarceration about the desperate privations of an American jail. As I listened to his gripes on the boring food, annoying gym routine and the crummy degree courses on offer, thought he was lucky to have drawn me. Had he met Pa, *he* would be suffering gunshot wounds from an indignant double-barrel by now.

Billy Barber's singsong rose and fell, swelling with menace. Wondered if he'd used up his one bullet, if he was trying for a heart attack.

Finally we both fell silent. I waited. For fifteen months I'd gone through my own private hell. Became destitute within forty-eight hours of fleeing Warri. Recognised the pickpocket team immediately. Other passengers avoided looking at my face. They? They avoided looking at my bag. They sat on either side of me and I resolved to watch them carefully, all nine hours of the trip to Potiskum.

Then the bus broke down, only eighty miles out of Warri. We were stranded on the barren roadside for nineteen hours while the driver to'd and fro'd as he tried to fix a broken valve in the engine. The sun was a merciless 33°C. The company was noisy and conflagrant. The two thieves took turns to sleep. Me? I kept my guard.

Bus fixed, we drove fifteen kilometres and the radiator exploded in a billow of steam. Tried to stop passing buses in vain. Another six hours passed before we were on the move again. I was stupid with sleep but I kept awake for hours before succumbing. Clawed up from stupor an hour after I must have dozed off. The bag under my feet had been slashed. My money was gone, as were both the boys. Went back to a relieved three-hour sleep before waking up to the reality of my destitution.

Had shaved past disaster and death so many times in the past few months. Thought I'd grown calluses. Which was partly why I returned: didn't care if the police came for me, didn't care if FazO's hoodlums came. Had quit running... yet, face-to-face with Billy Barber's righteous fury, I was deaf and dry-mouthed all over again.

I shut my eyes and waited.

Do you have a final request? He asked.

I kept my eyes closed as a tremor of hope passed through me. Of course I did! Could you kindly go away now! But I remained silent. *Do you have a final request?*

It was the voice, more than the words, much more than the hours he had spent working himself up for the kill, which told me he was no killer. He'd thought murderous thoughts, but he was no murderer. It was that thing Calamatus had said all over again: 'talking about killing, and killing, were two different countries entirely.' Perhaps Billy Barber could be provoked to murder, but his provocation was over a year old. Surely it was already too old to inspire cold blooded murder. I drew up the diary. I picked up a pen. I raised it to him.

Can I make a last entry? I'd like to bring this up to date for my son.

He nodded, and I bowed my head over the book. Somehow I knew that even visions of a burning National Library would not keep me from a final entry. Somehow I knew I could write forever. Slowly I began to write.

He was an African-American. That was the big surprise. Calama had swung a fishing rod over a river teeming with a hundred and ninety million white Americans only to hook another African like himself. Billy Barber was darker than I was, with classic Bantu features. Of course he had punched holes in his ear lobes and wore his hair in the same braids Patie used to favour. — And then there was the singsong voice. But I supposed that, after all the years, the ants that were smoked inside the fish would come to taste a little like the fish. But he sat there in the corner of my room as black and sarcastic as Meme Jumai himself. He was African alright.

Remembered FazO's rationale for his involvement in the 419 scams. Suddenly all his war-talk sounded a little hollow. He was duping the children of the slaves, not the children of the slavers.

Disconnected. That was what I was. Running from Tendu's corpse — I think that completely *unsocketed* me. Fifteen months I travelled northern Nigeria, eastern Cameroun and southern Chad. Rarely spent three weeks in one town, sometimes one day. Don't know for sure what drove me. A sense of perspective, most likely: a never looking forward beyond the next day. A never looking backwards beyond the last night... And every time I fled it became easier the next time...

Thirty days ago, was lounging at a street corner in Dadiya. Tuesday evening. Was across the street from the bakery where I worked. Was on the late shift, had just burned a batch of bread, and wasn't looking forward to resuming and facing the boss. Struck up a friendship with a passing tipper driver over a meal. He was hauling limestone to a cement factory up north. Talked him into a detour to get my bag. Didn't have much in the way of clothes, but I was building my savings in cash. Left Dadiya on that impulse — a burnt batch of bread — abandoning six days paid rent in an unplastered room, and four days' wages at the bakery.

He was chatty, that driver. Where're you really going? He'd asked.

North. I'd said.

That's a direction, not a destination. He'd said.

Which was when it hit me: if I didn't have a destination, I'd never really arrive.

Friendship with the driver lasted exactly three hours. Thirty kilometres out of town, he kindly pulled over to let me ease a full bladder. As soon as my zipper was down he drove off with my bag. It was the longest, most hopeless marathon I ever ran. Full bladder, cold, inky night, and no hope of ever catching him. Still, I ran some three kilometres before I stopped. Guess it was a kind of desperation, a burning-up of a passionate energy that, channelled elsewhere, would have endangered the continuation of my life. I was back where I started, without even a slashed bag or a change of clothes this time.

Managed to get through that night.

What kept me going? Perhaps the cowardice I grew in hospital after the car-crash that cost Tendu his leg. Perhaps a sense of history: the determination not to countenance the final Grand Gesture Pa and Calama had so favoured. The conviction that I would have a life after disaster, no matter how circumscribed.

What *really* kept me going? Finally, a destination down south. I would flee no more. Whether Meme Jumai was my biological father or not, he was *Pa*. And whether Ikerre-Oti was my hometown or not, it was *home*. I had searched out its history. I *knew* it. Back there was a patch of land with my name on it. It was the only land I could claim on the earth without being lynched as a thief. It was within hailing distance from a stream, had a house on it, and farmland, which had once raised a family.

But by dawn I found the cause of the eerie snorting that had gone on through the night. A herd of three dozen or so cows were bellied down in the grassy valley, three hundred metres from the road. Where there was a herd, there'd be herdsmen. Thinking to beg a bus fare, or at the most wretched, company for the long trek south, I struck out across the savanna towards the herd.

Only then did I notice the hawks and the vultures circling low. Saw his bundle on the ledge. Found Abdul doubled up in the ditch below. Broken right leg twice as big as the healthy left one. Was unconscious till I touched him. Had stumbled into the ravine several days earlier. High fever. Semi-delirious. Dehydrated... I carried him out of the ditch. His courage humbled me. Sight of his wound made me gag, but *he* was cracking jokes. Got him under a tree, away from the rising sun. His flask was empty. On his directions, followed the valley six kilometres to a stream that had shrunk to a pond. In the distance, some thirty minutes trek beyond the water, I saw the gleaming zinc roofs of a small town.

He was still alive when I returned. Drank thirstily. He summoned a cow and milked her when I couldn't. I scavenged for fruits for him and I. The fever was burning him up, but he wanted a fire. Gathered the kindling and wood. As dusk fell, set them alight. He described some herbs which grew mostly by streams and ponds. I found them. Impossible to get him to the road with the state of his leg. Impossible to stop a vehicle for a hospital run either. The smell from his leg was foul, though nowhere near as foul as the herbs when they were boiling in a can from his bundle. It was a trial merely to stand there, watching him drink some, and pour the rest over the filthy poultice on his gangrenous leg.

He was delirious half the time. Rest of the time, he was telling me his life story. Never built such an intense relationship in such a short space of time. Guess it was the death in the air. He was well over sixty but not quite seventy. Patriach of a family of herdsmen. Father and grandfather before him were nomadic herdsmen, but his three sons were right prodigals; They'd taken their portions of his herd, sold them off, and pursued a wasteful, sedentary lifestyle as Dadiya security-men. His last wife had died several years before.

Abdul's medicine did him no good. He must have known I was actually attending his wake. Dusk fell.

Make sure the vultures don't get my flesh. He said, over and over again.

His flesh and his cows. Those were his prime concerns. He had a roll of naira notes in his bundle, a few hundreds, which he gave to me. It would be enough to get me to Lokoja before I'd have to beg again... He made me promise to deliver his cows to his sons. I'd never driven a cow in my life, but he expected me to drive three dozen animals 30 kilometres to the very town I'd just fled. I humoured him. He demonstrated the clicks, the calls. I wasn't to fear the horns. Was to show some authority and they'd fall in line. Was like bike-riding: any old idiot could do it. His sons would be forced by necessity to return to the family business... They'd reward me handsomely for my pains. His cows were like family. Their forbears had belonged to his own forbears for eight to nine generations.

And they all carried marks recognisable by every cattle dealer between Zigey and Lokoja... people had been lynched for selling cattle that did not belong to them...

As night fell, his good humour failed. His silence became brooding. He began to see several people walking around our tree. With one man who smelt of locust beans, he argued a complex fiscal transaction. He seemed prepared to pay off the debt at once. Wasn't sure the offer was accepted. With another visitor he was wheedling: how could he spend a lifetime driving cattle from desert to grasslands to forests, and he couldn't even take one across. Finally he seemed to give up and dropped off to sleep. I rolled several feet away from the odious smell. Tried to sleep myself. An hour had passed before his movement woke me up. But it was such a furtive movement that I remained still. He was loosening a leather belt from under his clothes. He surreptitiously slipped it off. He placed it in the fire and stoked it up.

He was dead by dawn. Among the cold ashes, found a bulging money belt half-charred in the fire. Most of the currency notes were ruined. What wasn't still amounted to a small fortune.

You could know a man intensely for twelve hours and not know him at all.

Left his body to the vultures.

Took Abdul's crook. Applied it angrily. Fired by rage, I overcame my morbid fear of the massive animals — *which carried marks on their rumps recognisable by every cattle dealer between Zigey and Lokoja.* Overcame my fear of their large, knowing eyes, their menacing horns, and the possibility of a death by lynching. Drove them south towards the stream and the settlement I spied beyond. The further I got from the corpse under the tree, the more futile seemed an anger that burned against a cadaver but couldn't penetrate the grave. Further I walked away from the tree, more time I had to wonder why it fell upon one man in one lifetime to stumble upon the corpses of two itinerants. The first one I permitted Calama to desecrate for a nickname. The second I was leaving to the vultures to desecrate, for what? Further I walked, the more I felt I was abandoning Pa's bones once again.

Left the cattle a kilometre to the stream. Trekked back to Abdul's corpse. Drove away the ungainly birds. Dug a shallow grave under the tree with his cutlass. Lay him flat. Clothed him with earth. Perspiring like mad when I finished; but some of the drops on the ground were tears. Suddenly it was no longer difficult to grieve for Pa. — Grieved not just for a nomadic drover who tried to take it with him, but for all those possessed of family who met the desolation of death alone.

The cows had found the stream when I returned. Two cows had calved recently. Couldn't get them and their charges to leave the water. Had to head out without them. Lost seven more recalcitrants on the way to the town that turned out to be Sema. Found the slaughterhouse on the outskirts. Beside it was a cattle market. Bargained with a dealer who looked closely at the rumps of the cattle. There was a moment when I thought I was going to end up between two tyres like my father, then I mentioned my asking price, which was a good fraction lower than the cattle was worth.

He called in three other dealers and they huddled in a secretive discussion. Once again, furtive glances were thrown my way. Then I mentioned that Abdul probably suspected there wasn't enough money in Sema's cattle market, when he suggested to me to take them to his sons in Dadiya. That did the trick. They dug into their boxes. Forty-eight hours after my second destitution, I was richer than I had ever been in my life. Had the means to go anywhere, do anything...

Still chose to retire to Ikerre-Oti, to the devils I knew. I had made the decision broke. I'd keep it now that I was rich. Was still somewhat apprehensive about the threat of death that I had fled from, but now I had seen the difference between living and being alive.

Guess I was lost in the diary. An hour must have passed since I bent over it. Had been prepared to write for days, if stopping would switch off my lights. But my hands were trembling now with nervous energy. It wasn't the number of words I had written. It was the violence with which they were coming. Was reaching that terrible crux of months ago, when I was guarding my bag from the pickpockets in the bus out of Warri: I finally became pleased to lose my money — if only I could finally sleep at last. I was getting ready to do anything to break the tension cracking me up.

Suddenly, I was startled back into the present by a ragged snore. Glanced up incredulously. Billy Barber had gold fillings in several molars! Under the table, I slipped off my shoes noiselessly. Hesitated. If he had dallied this long because he wasn't angry enough to kill, could an escape attempt provide the provocation to pull the trigger? Could I take the risk? Wet with sweat. But for the farcical snoring of the sleeping assassin, it was a silent night in Ikerre-Oti... and I think I can hear Opportunity clearly.

I'll just get the door...